THE SECRETS: VOLUME ONE

THE OTHER STATUE

Edward Gorey

BLOOMSBURY

First published in Great Britain 2002

Copyright © 1968 by Edward Gorey

The moral right of the author has been asserted

Bloomsbury Publishing Plc, 38 Soho Square,
London W1D 3HB

A CIP catalogue record for this book
is available from the British Library

ISBN 0 7475 6084 6

10 9 8 7 6 5 4 3 2 1

Printed in Singapore by Tien Wah Press

Homage to Jane Austen

The autumn tints of 19__ were at their most brilliant for the annual charity fête on the grounds of Backwater Hall in Mortshire.

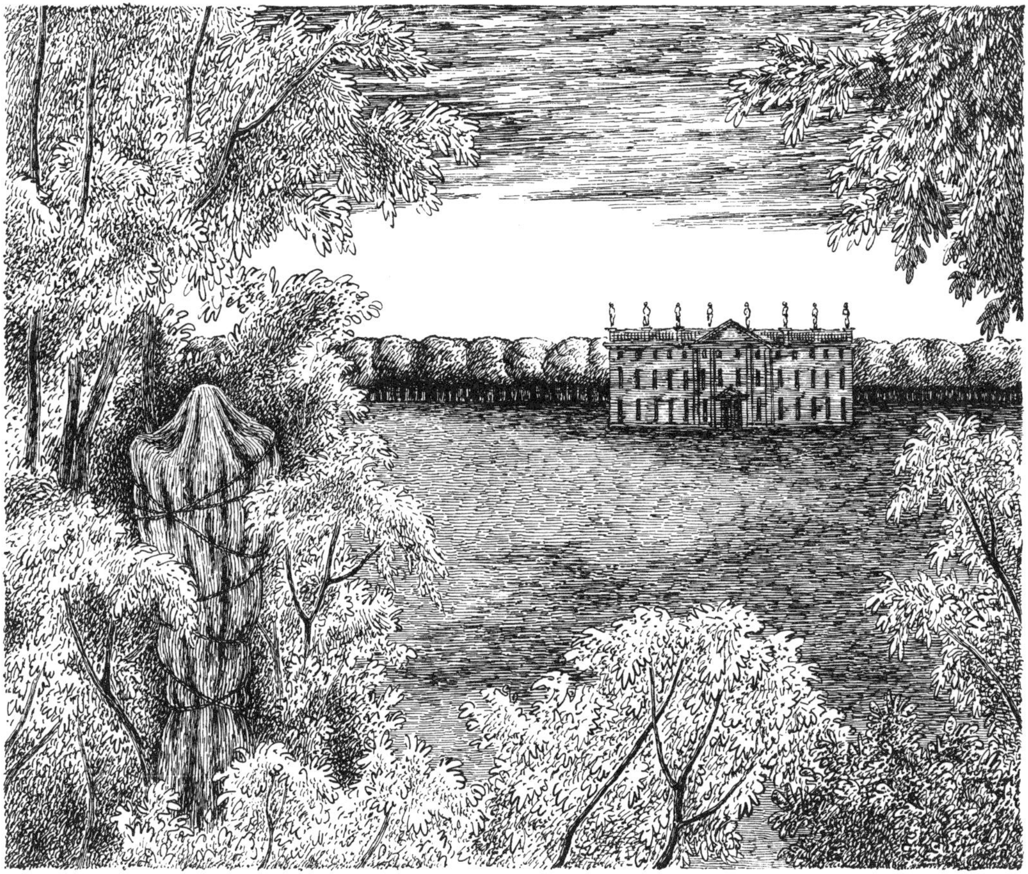

After luncheon Miss Underfold, the governess, waited until the Earl of Thump and Lady Emily Lisping were taking their naps before slipping away from the nursery.

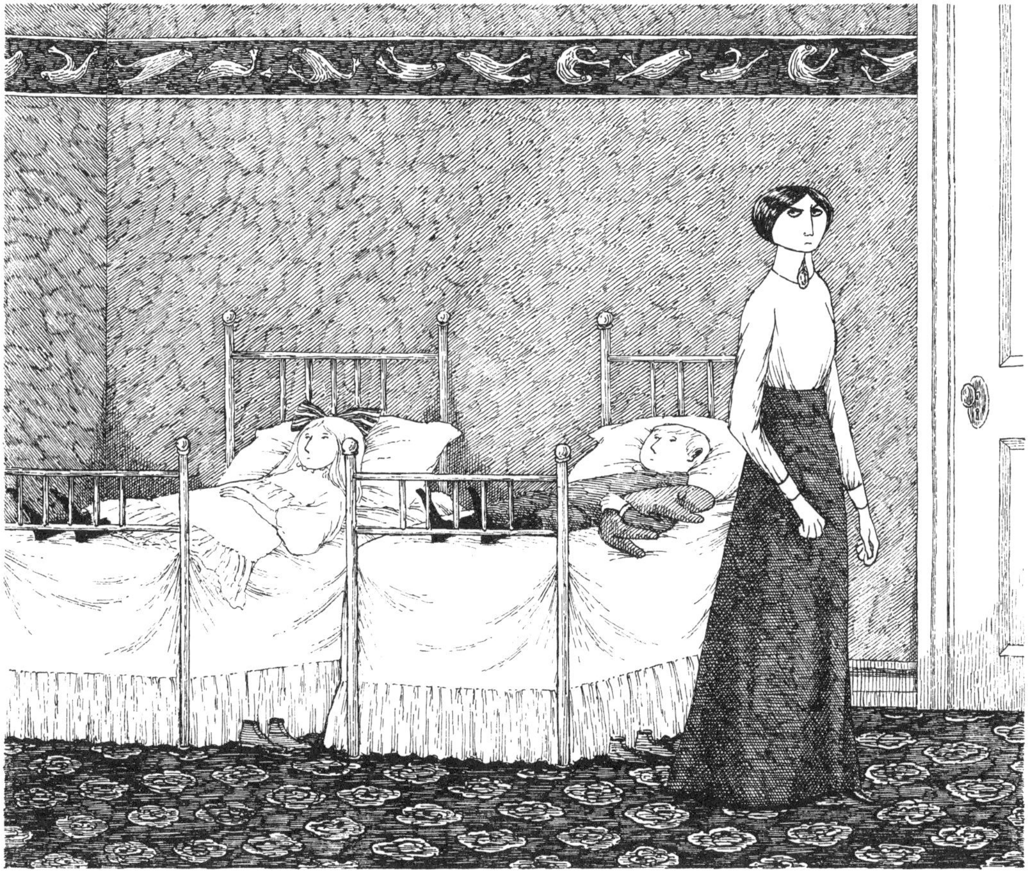

A gypsy selling Orphobismic Lozenges was told to remove himself by Fenks, the butler, as the first guests neared the gates.

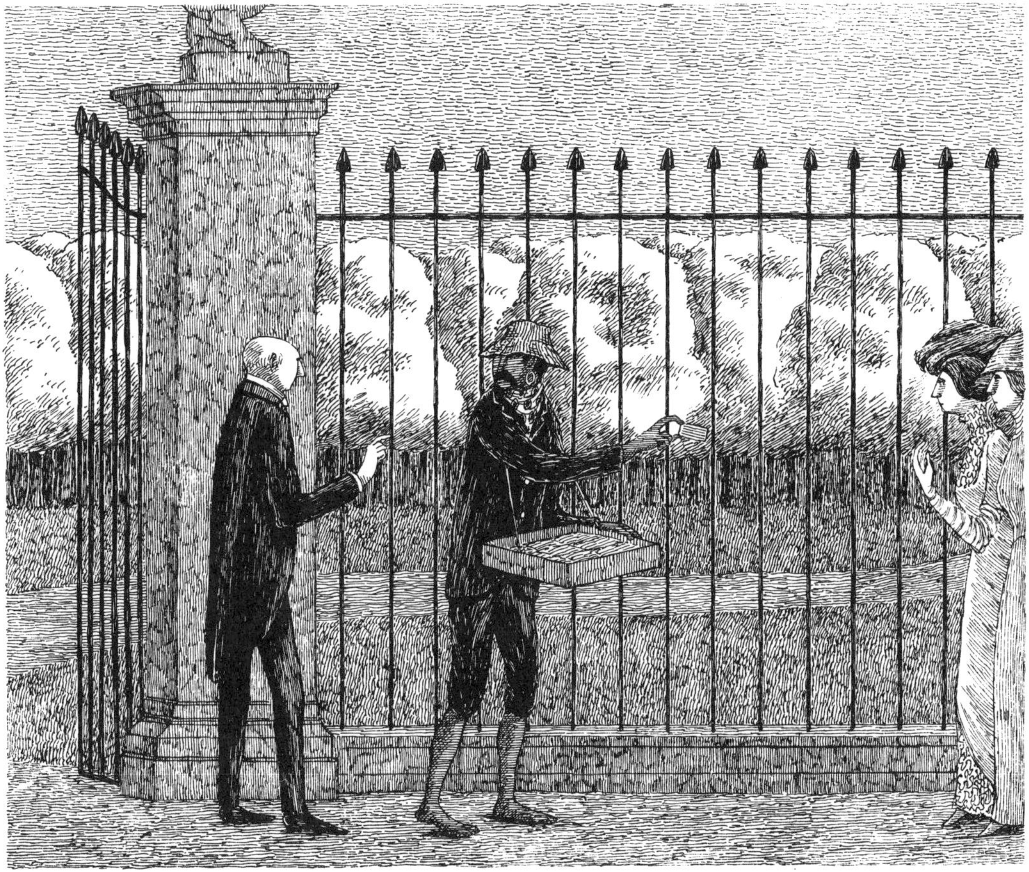

Lady Flora, his elder daughter, discovered the Marquess of Wherewithal on the terrace, peering upwards.

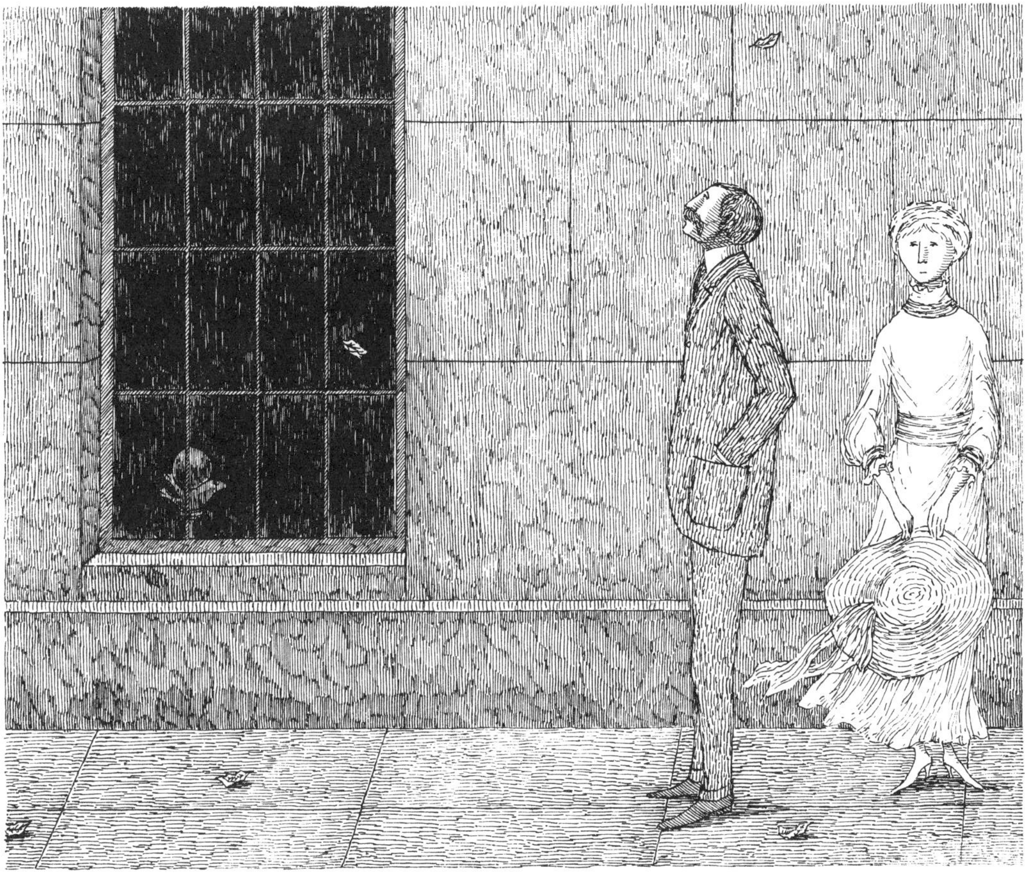

The gypsy was nowhere to be seen by the time Horace Gollop turned into the drive.

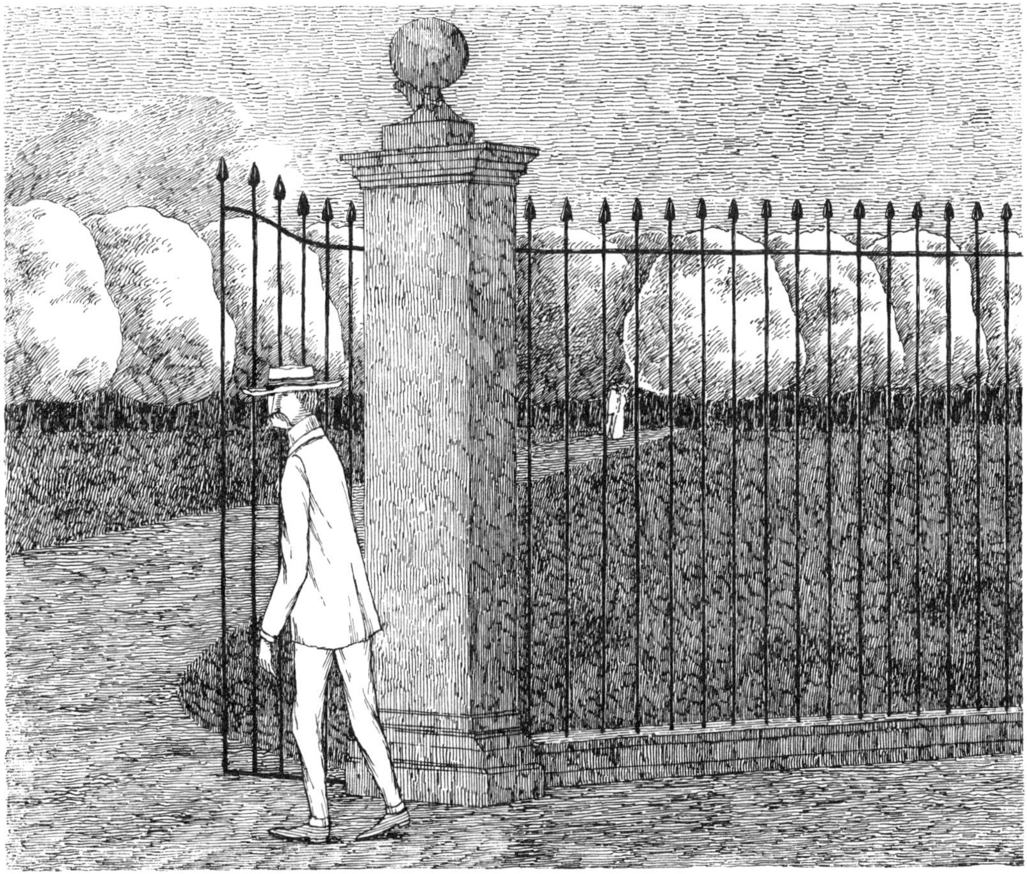

He was recognized at once by Lady Isobel Stringless, Lord Wherewithal's aunt, although they had last met seventeen years before on St Clot in the Maladroit Islands.

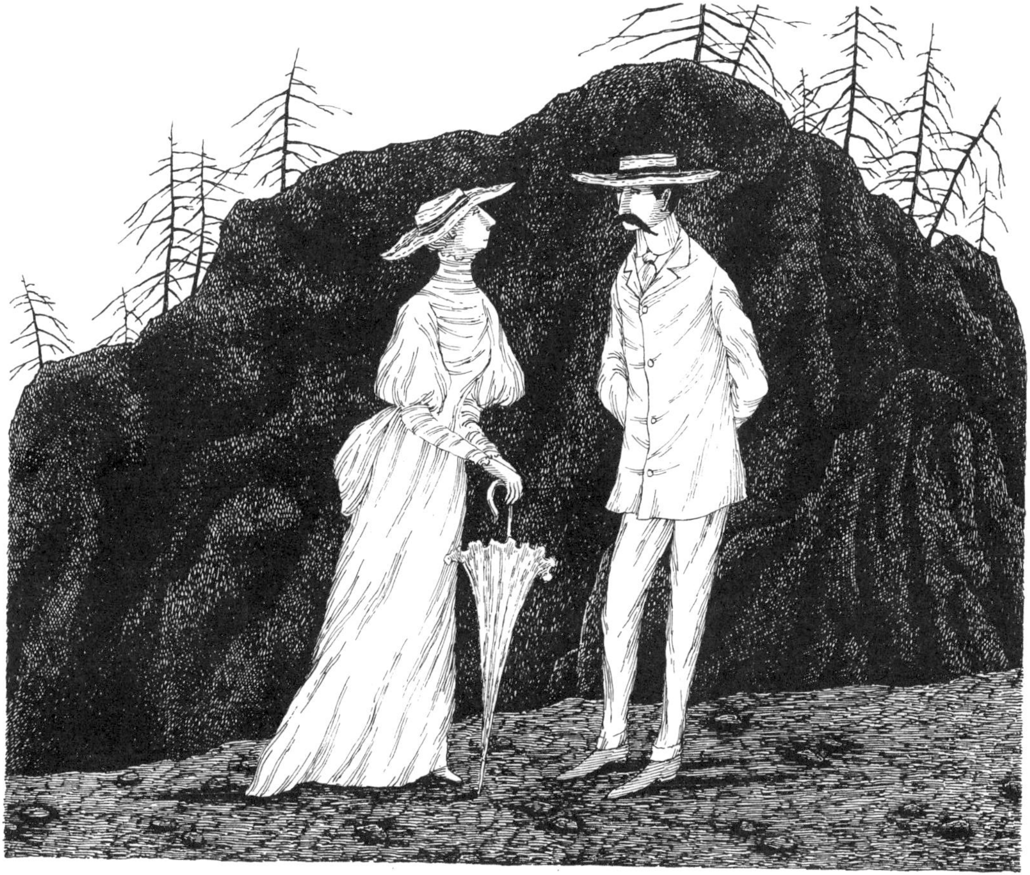

A clergyman staying at the Upturned Pig, the Rev. O. MacAbloo, wandered in a remote corner of the shrubbery.

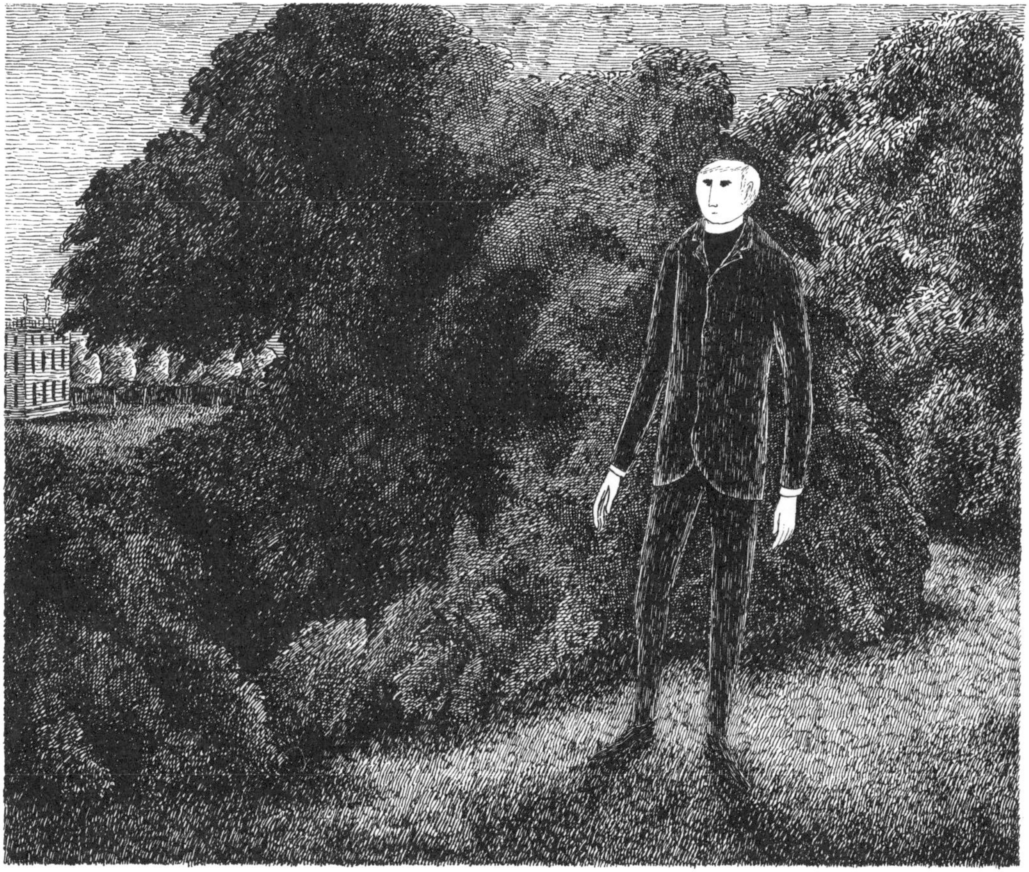

Augustus woke up to find his stuffed twisby was missing.

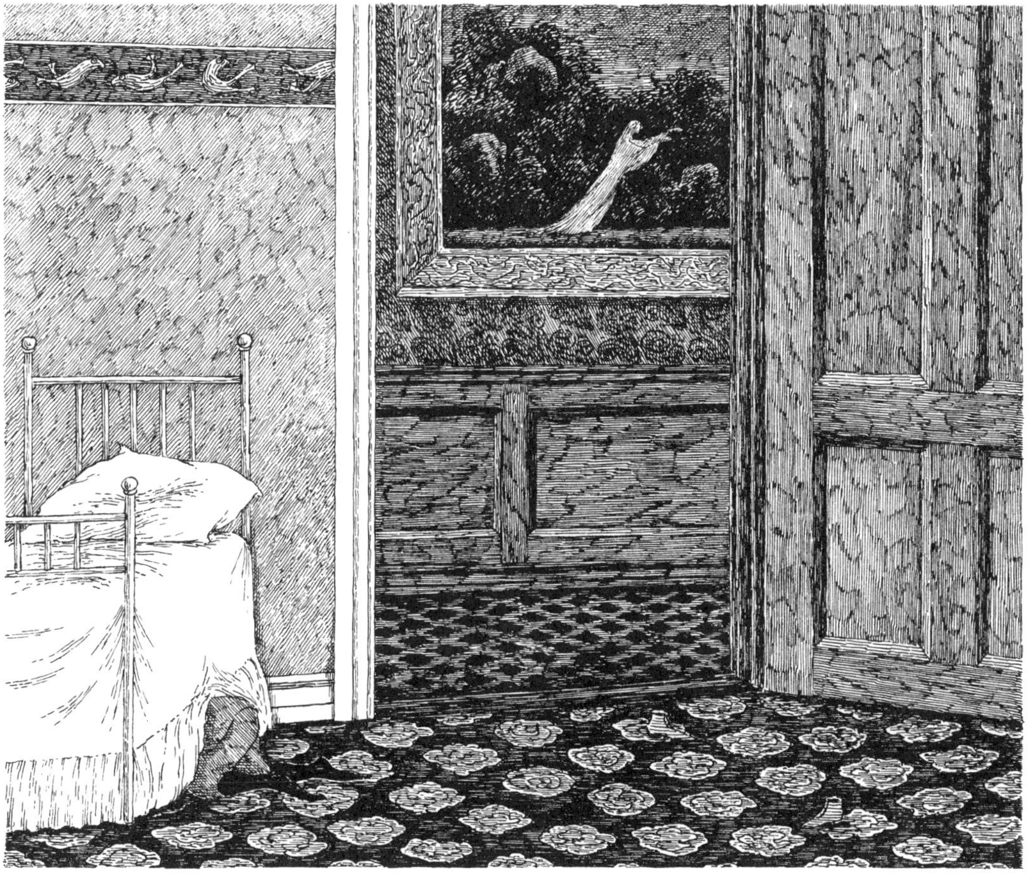

Something went wrong with Dr Maximilian Belgravius's motor on the far side of the village.

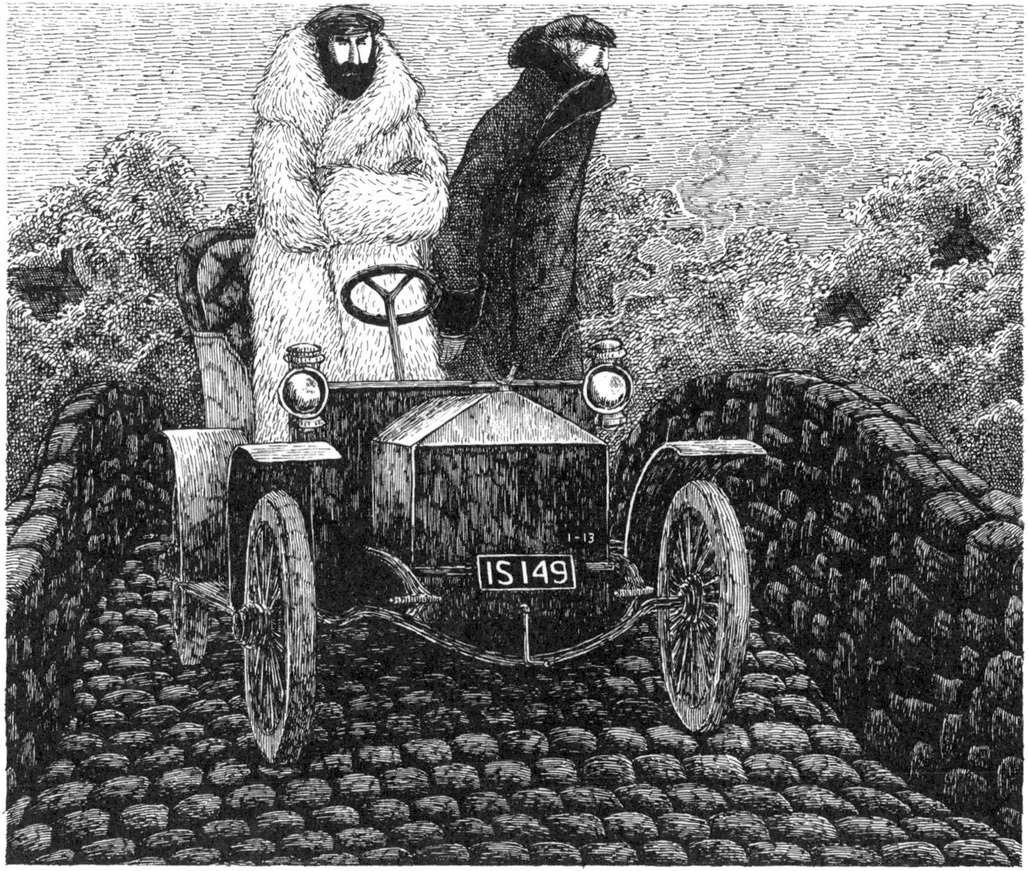
1-13
IS149

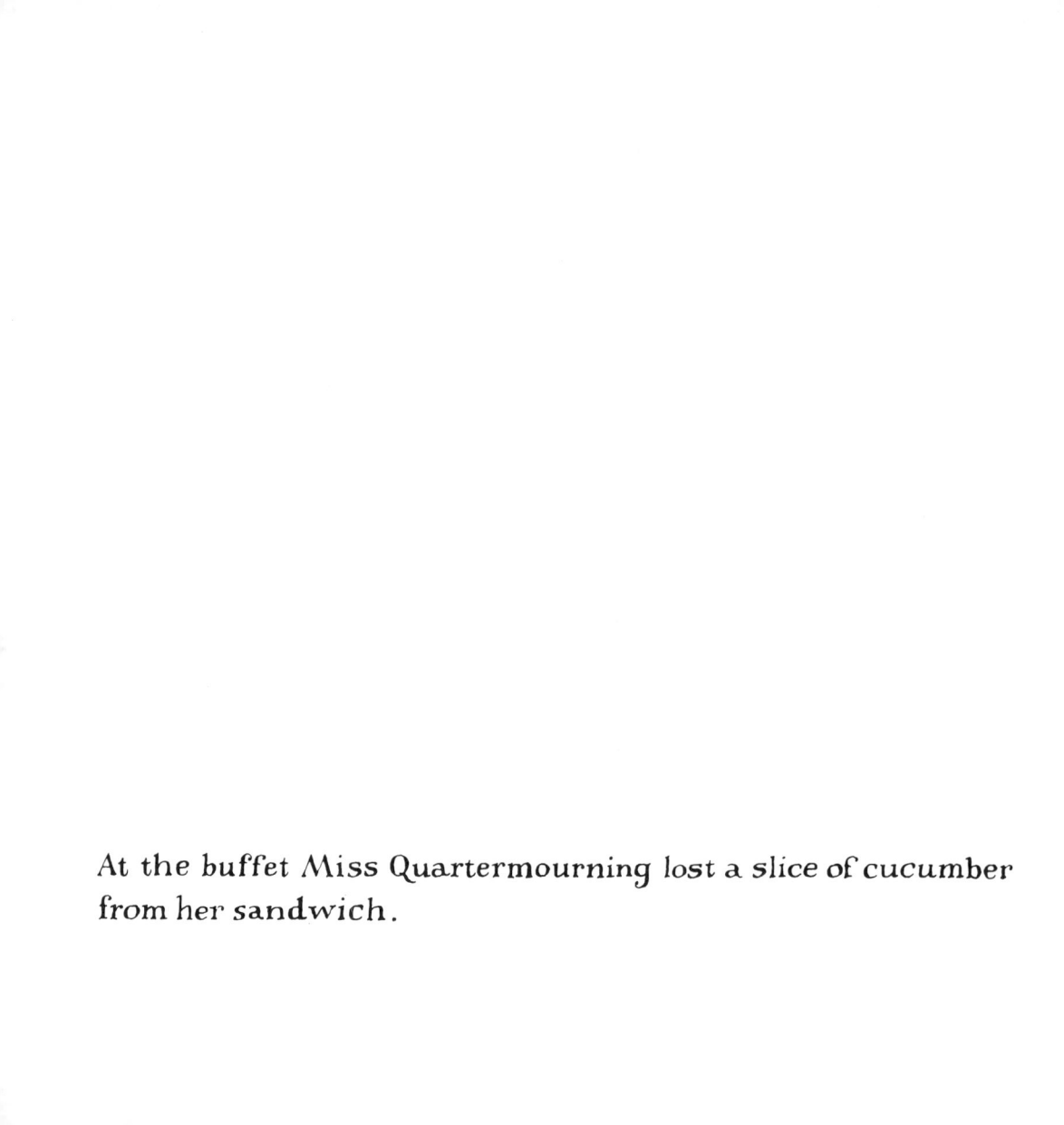

At the buffet Miss Quartermourning lost a slice of cucumber from her sandwich.

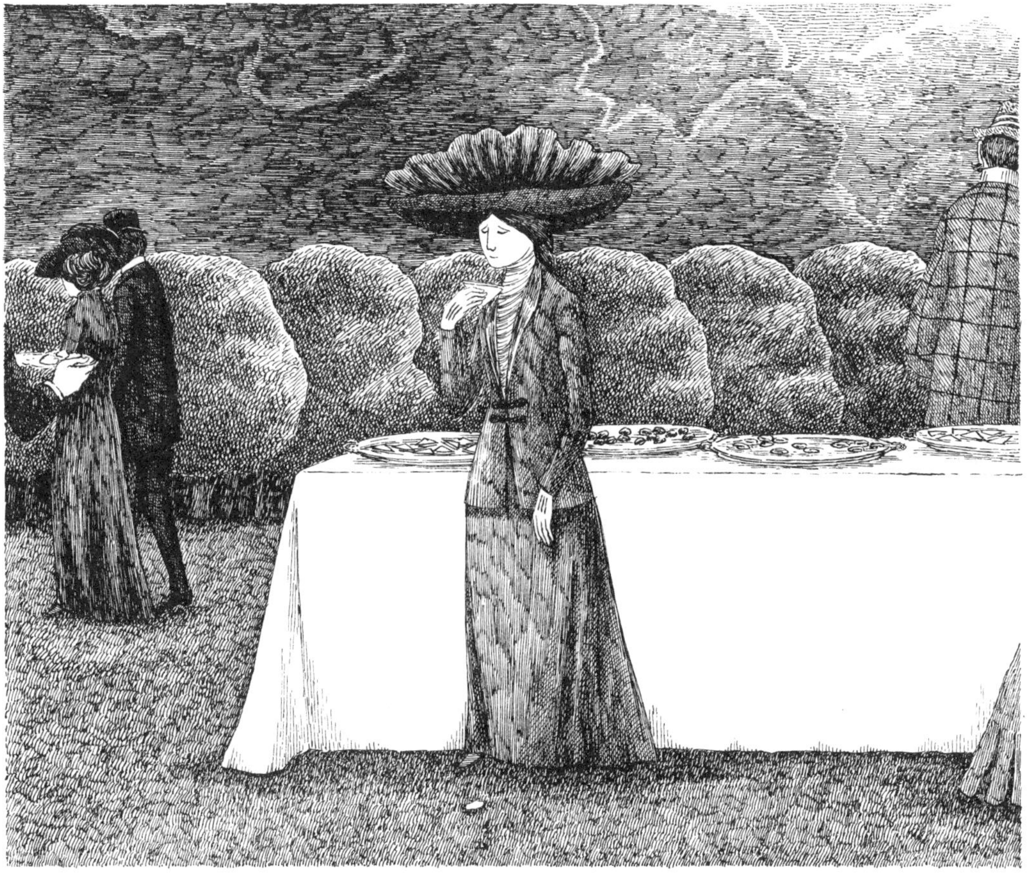

A sudden gust of wind came up from nowhere and rushed through the trees.

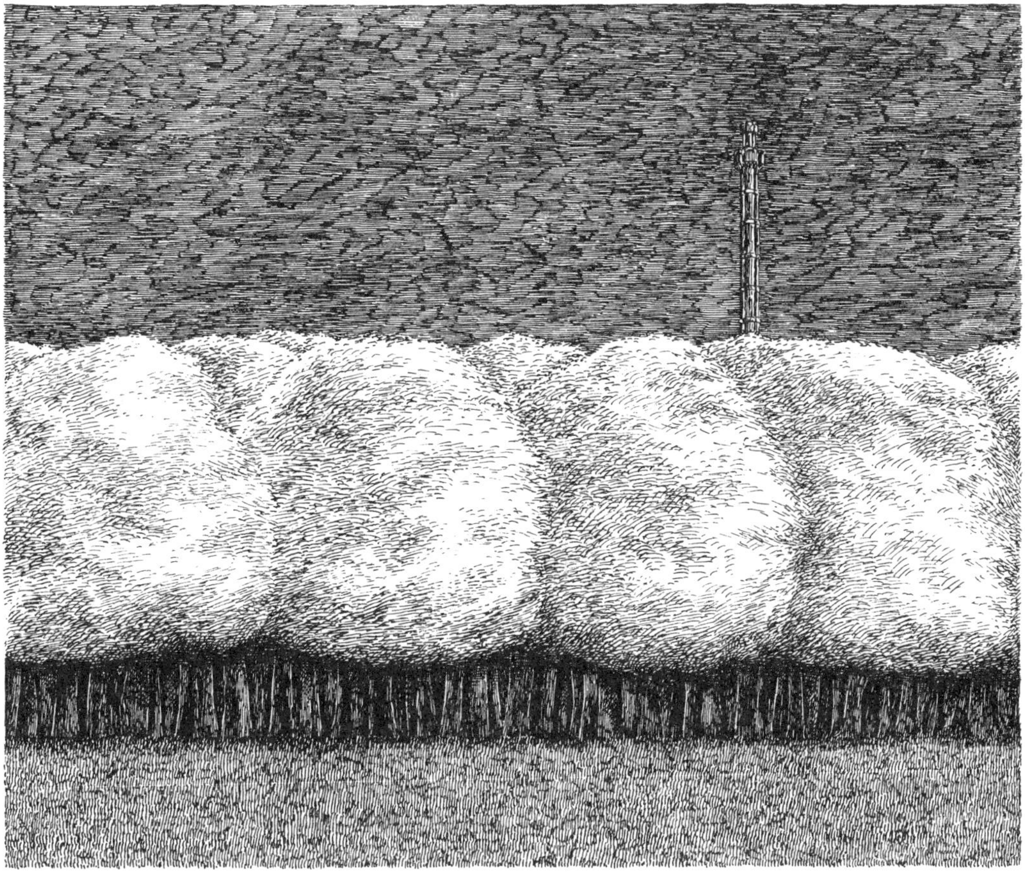

After it had passed, Lord Wherewithal was found crushed beneath a statue blown down from the parapet.

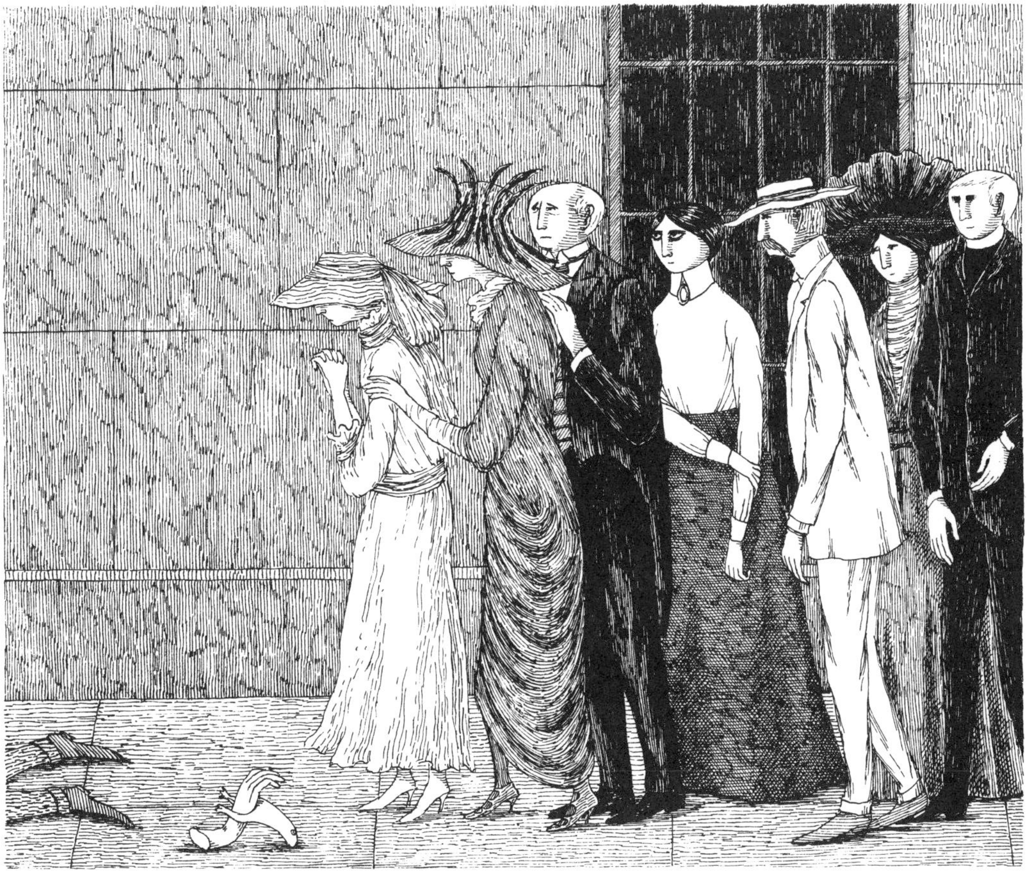

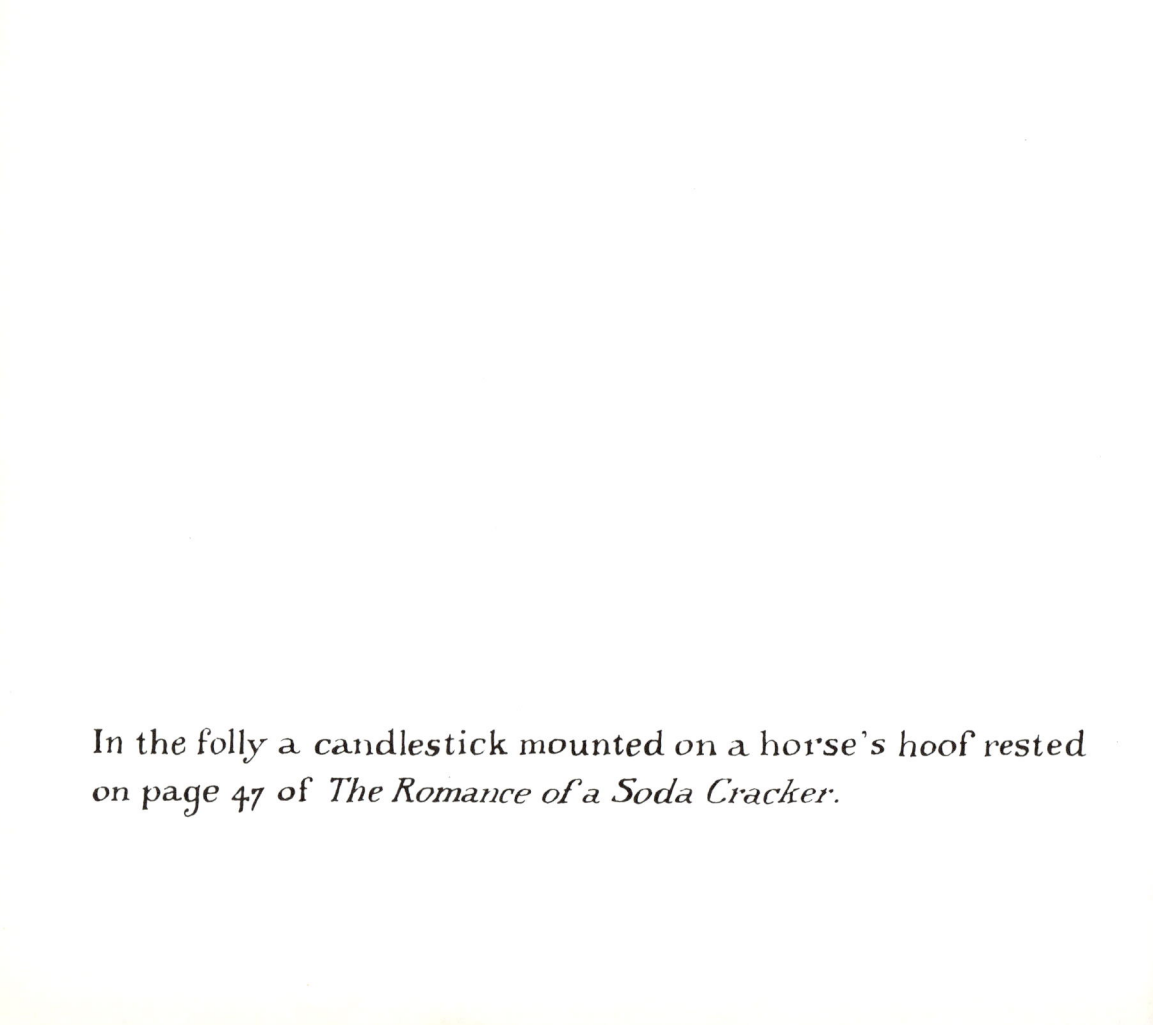

In the folly a candlestick mounted on a horse's hoof rested on page 47 of *The Romance of a Soda Cracker*.

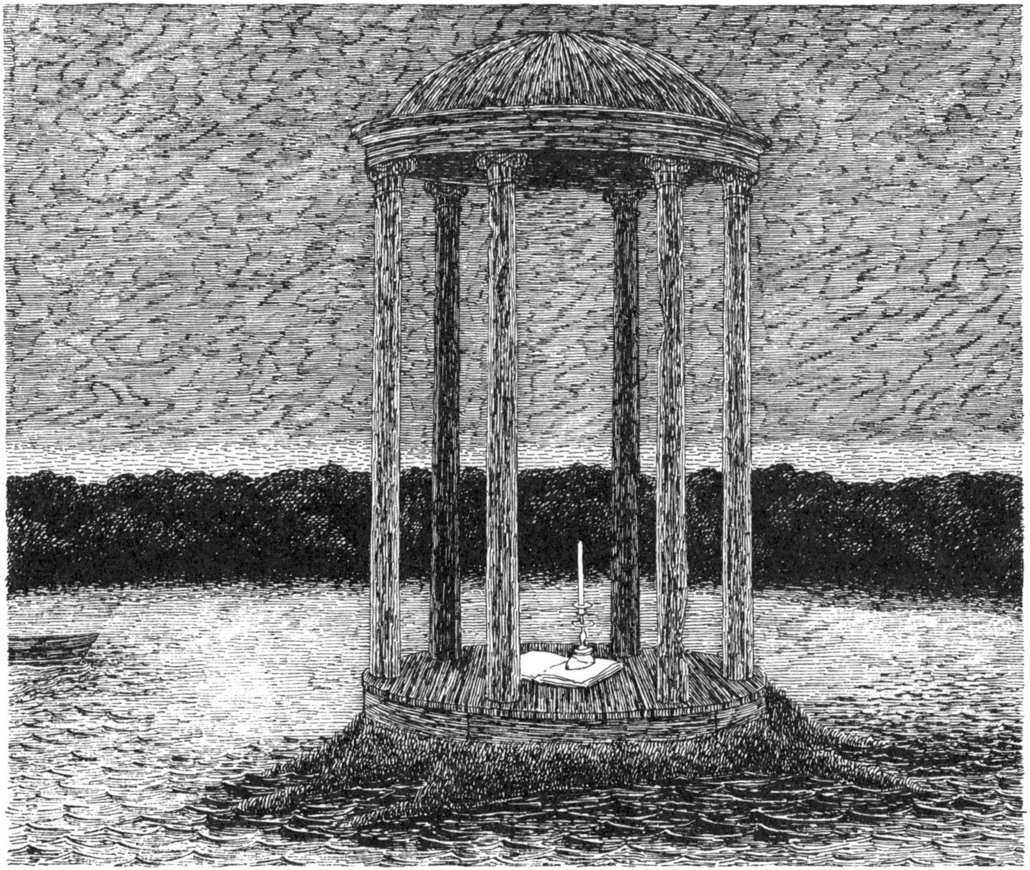

Dr Belgravius and his nephew, Luke Touchpaper, drove up as the body was being taken indoors.

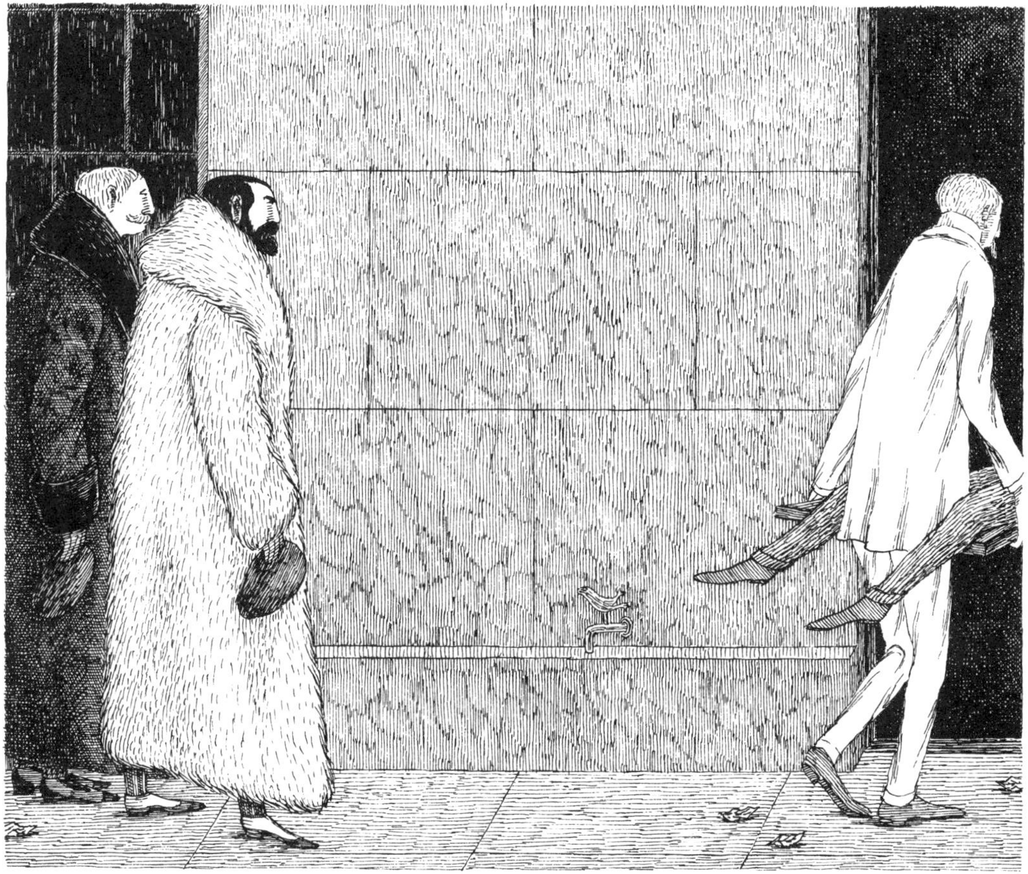

The fête broke up in confusion and dismay.

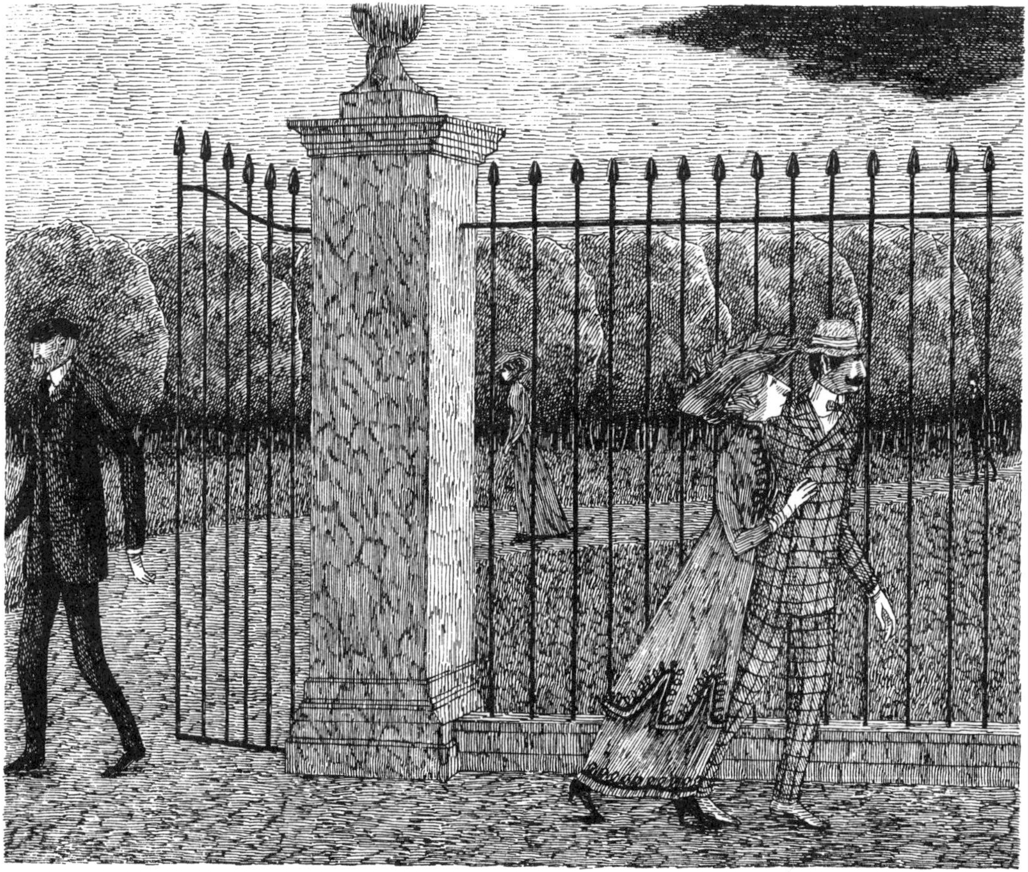

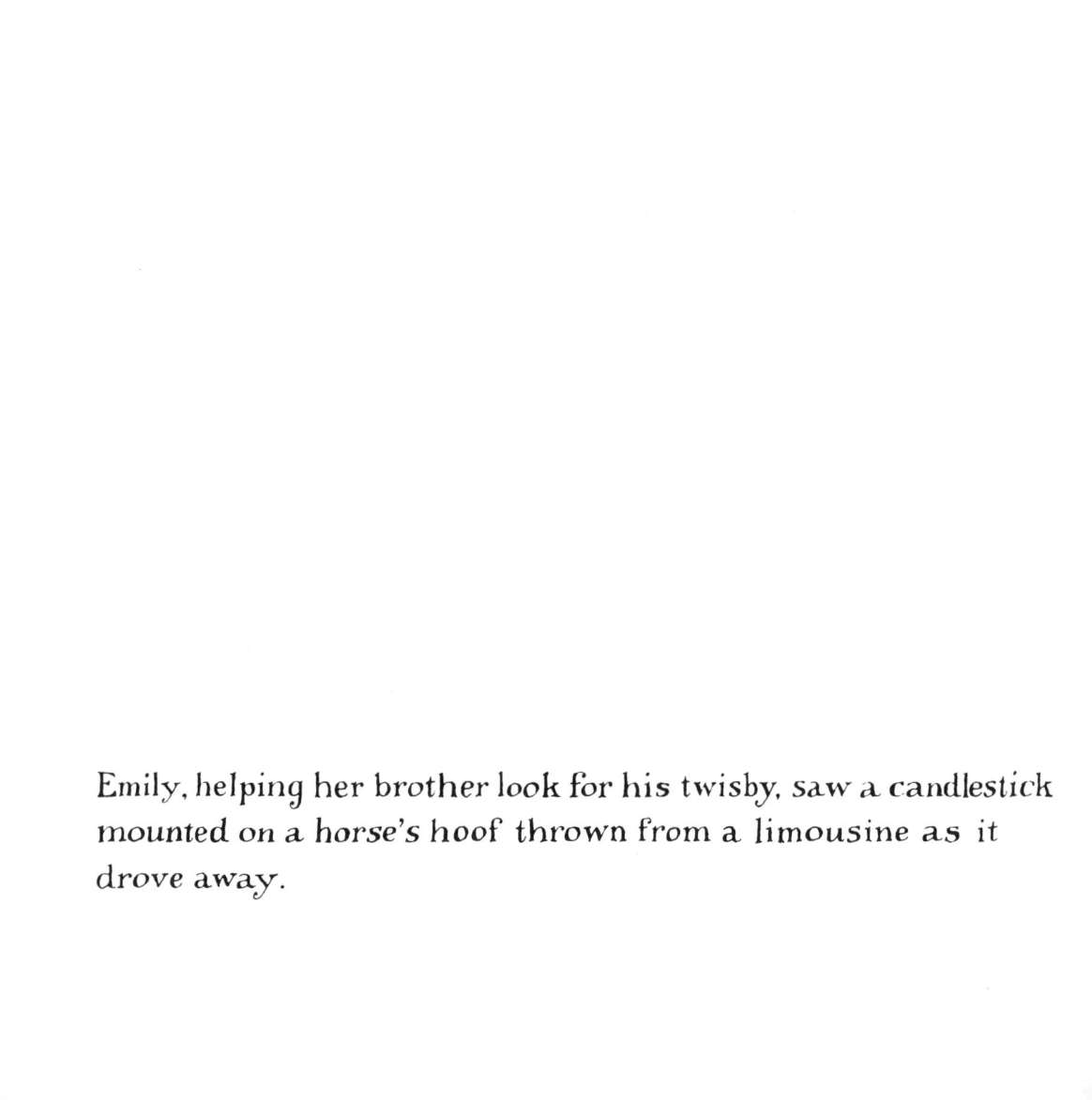

Emily, helping her brother look for his twisby, saw a candlestick mounted on a horse's hoof thrown from a limousine as it drove away.

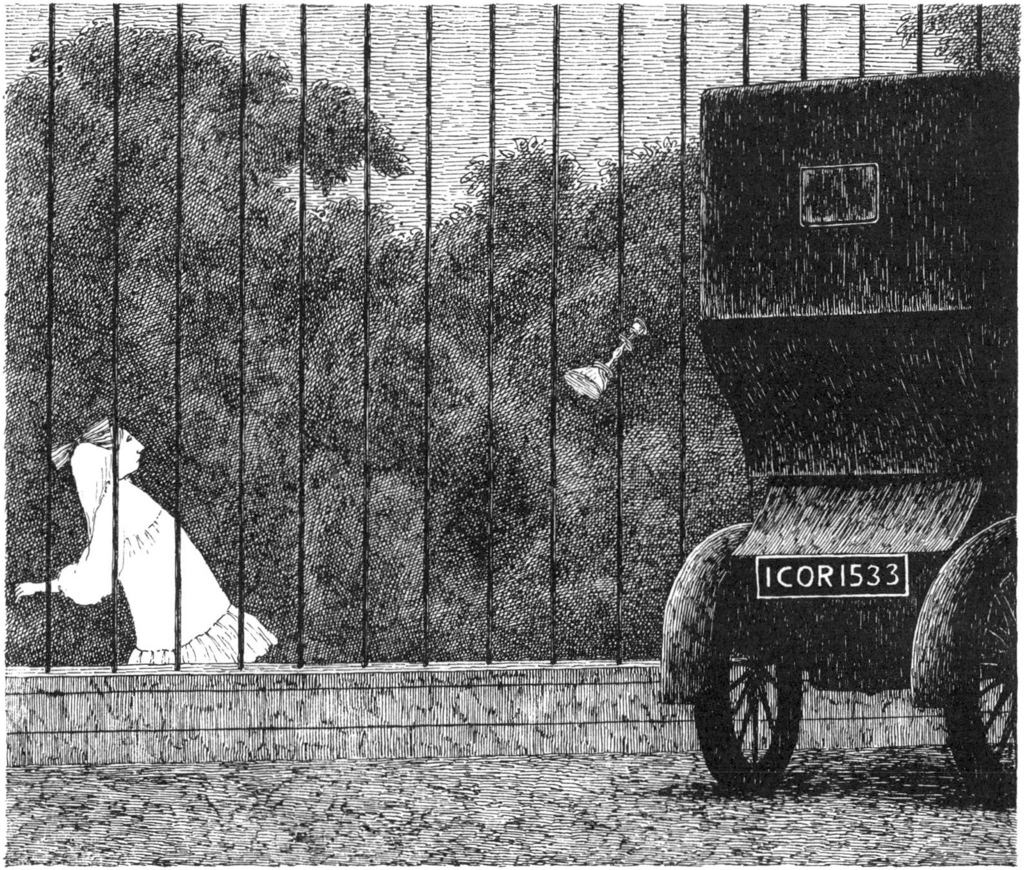
ICOR1533

On the roof a curious discovery was made.

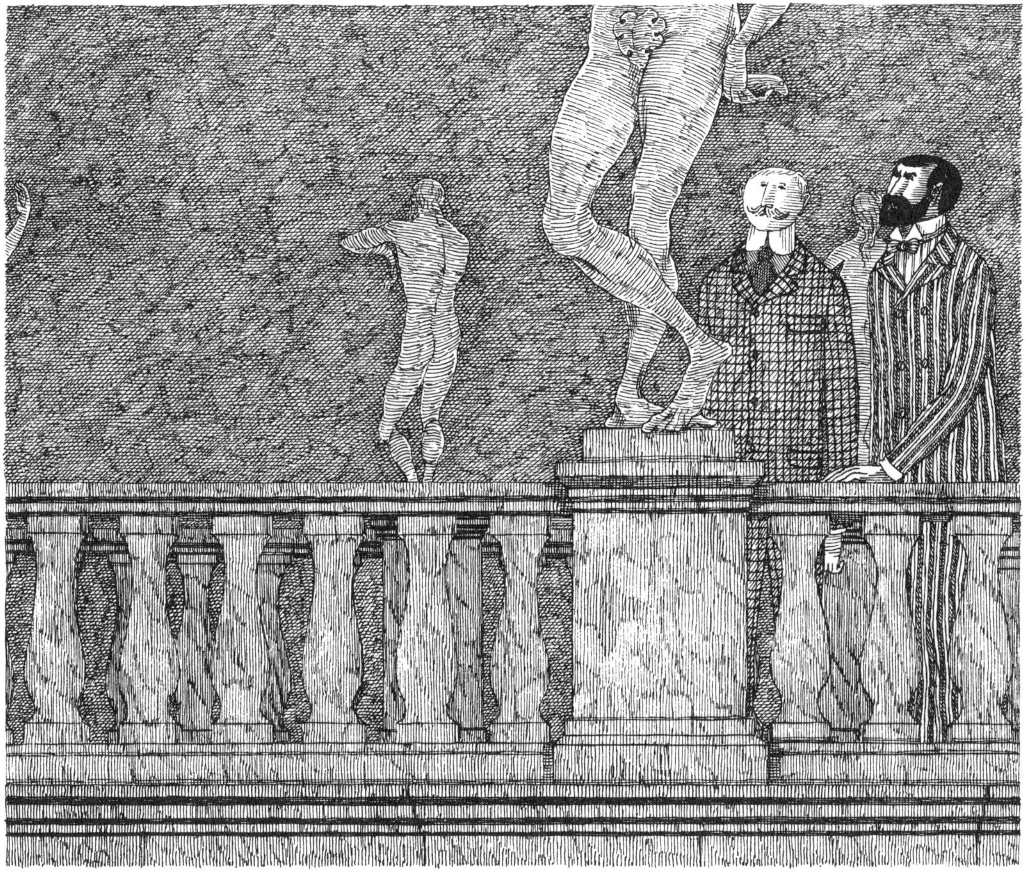

As the party was about to retire for the night Fenks announced that the Lisping Elbow was not in its case.

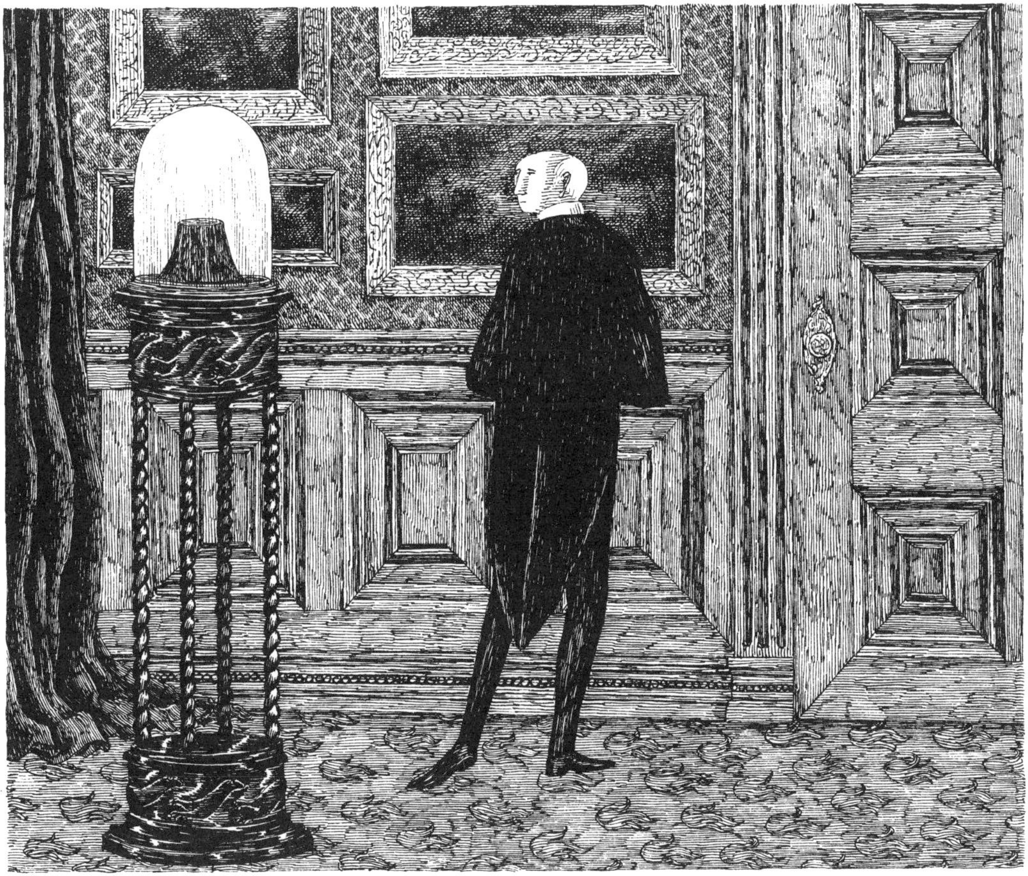

The family was baffled: though their oldest heirloom, it was only made of wax and of no value to anyone else.

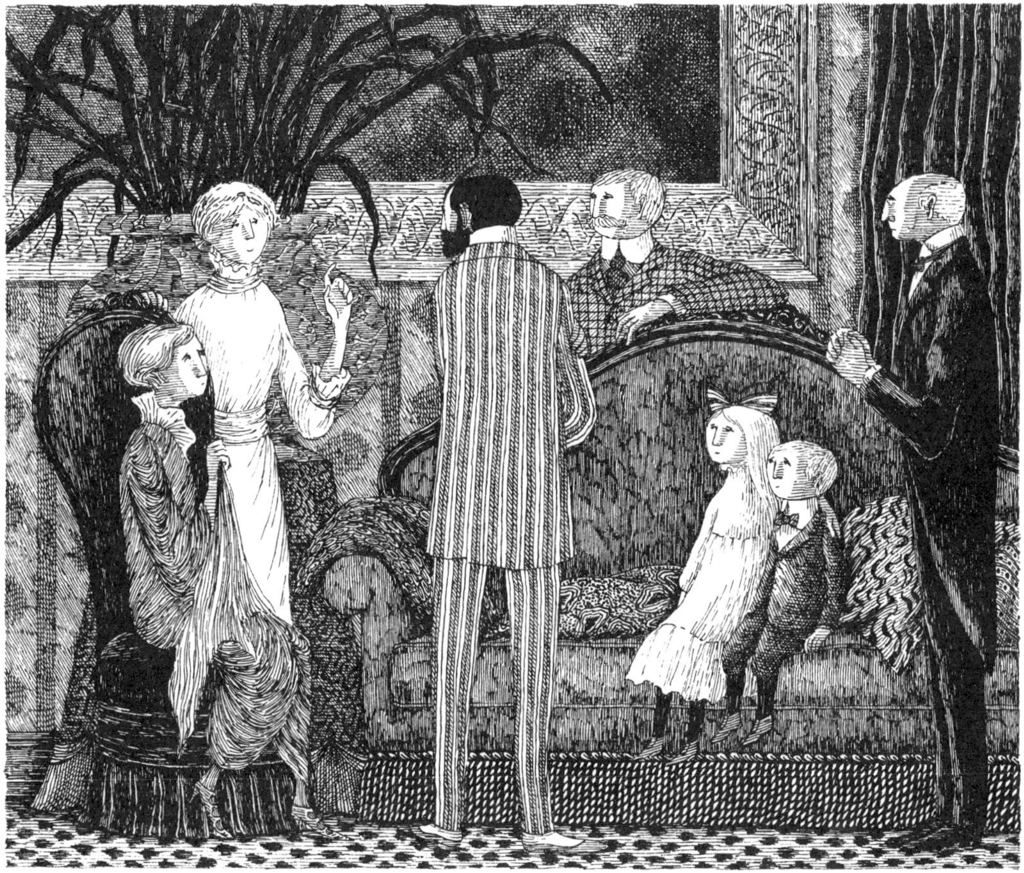

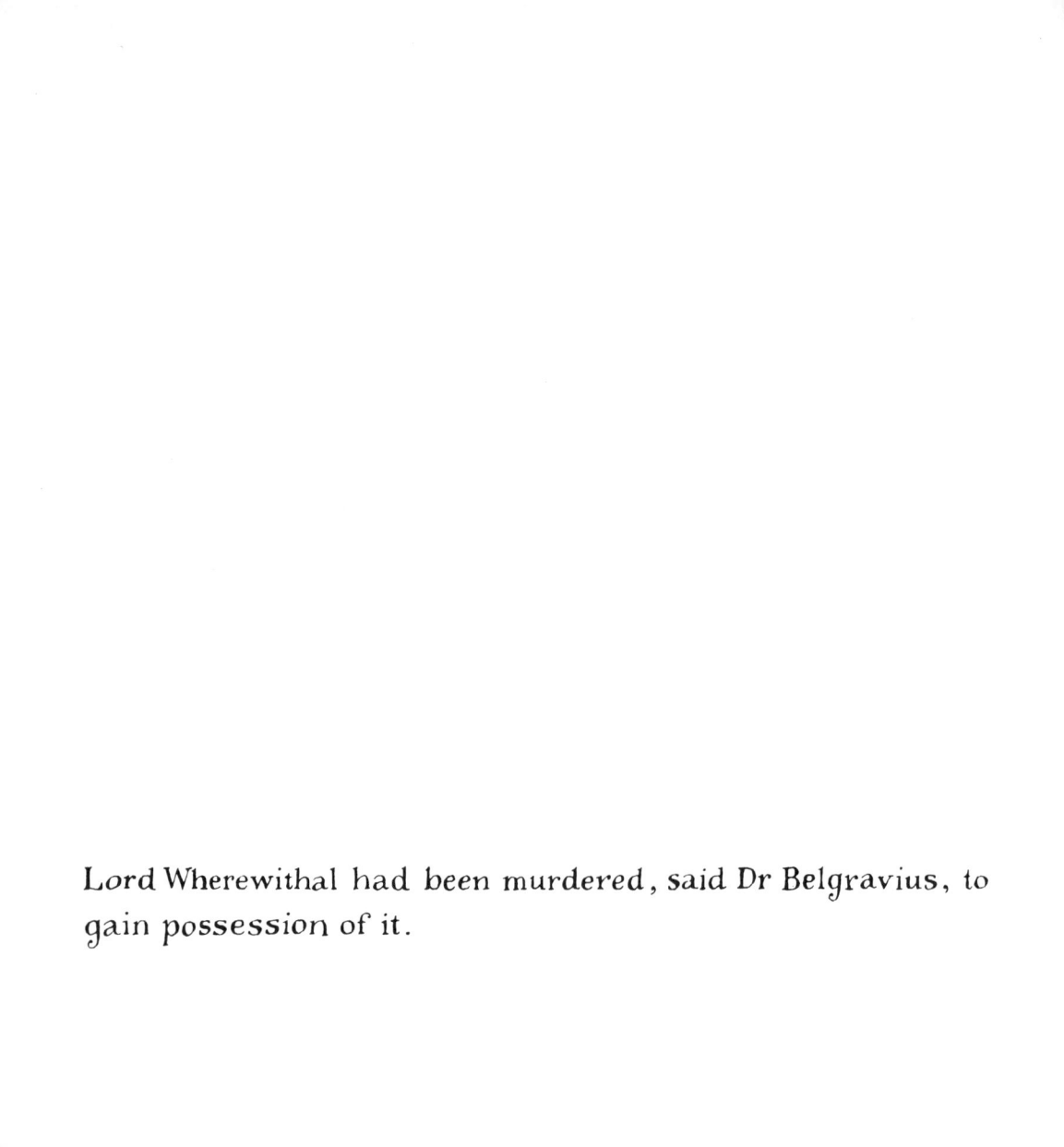

Lord Wherewithal had been murdered, said Dr Belgravius, to gain possession of it.

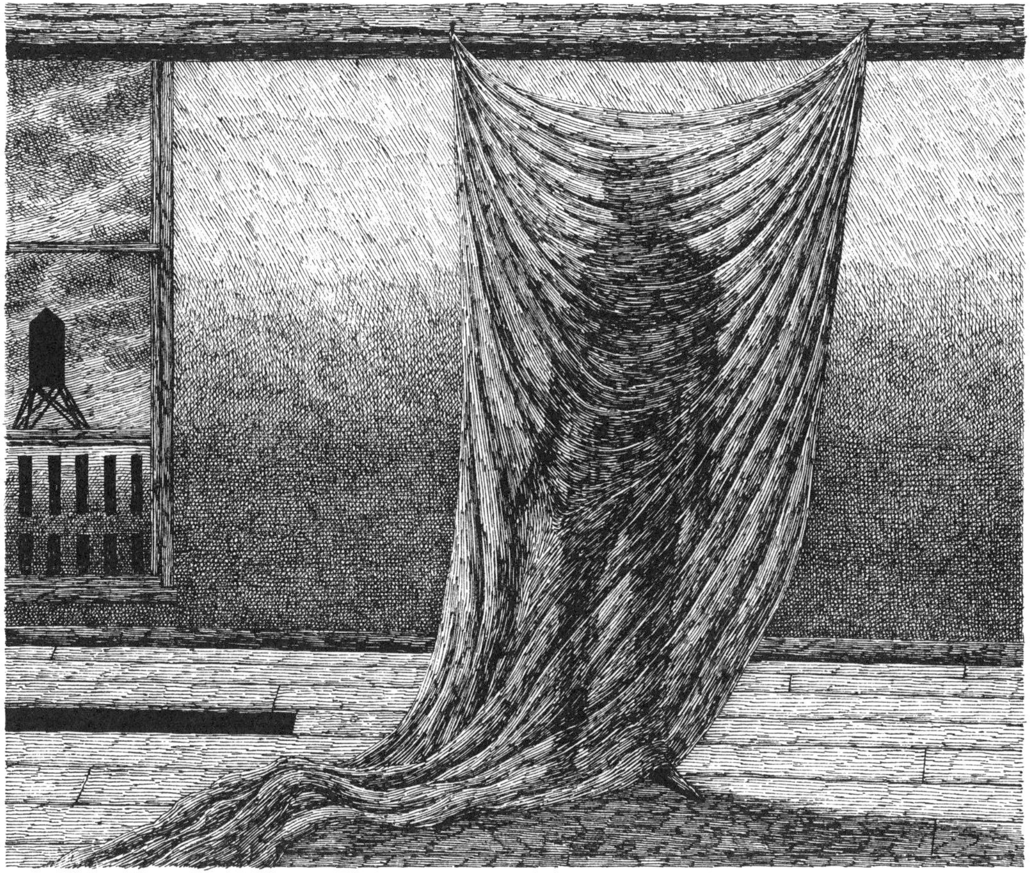

Due to the indisposition of both the vicar and his curate, the burial-service was taken by Mr MacAbloo.

HERE LYES BURIED
THE BODY OF

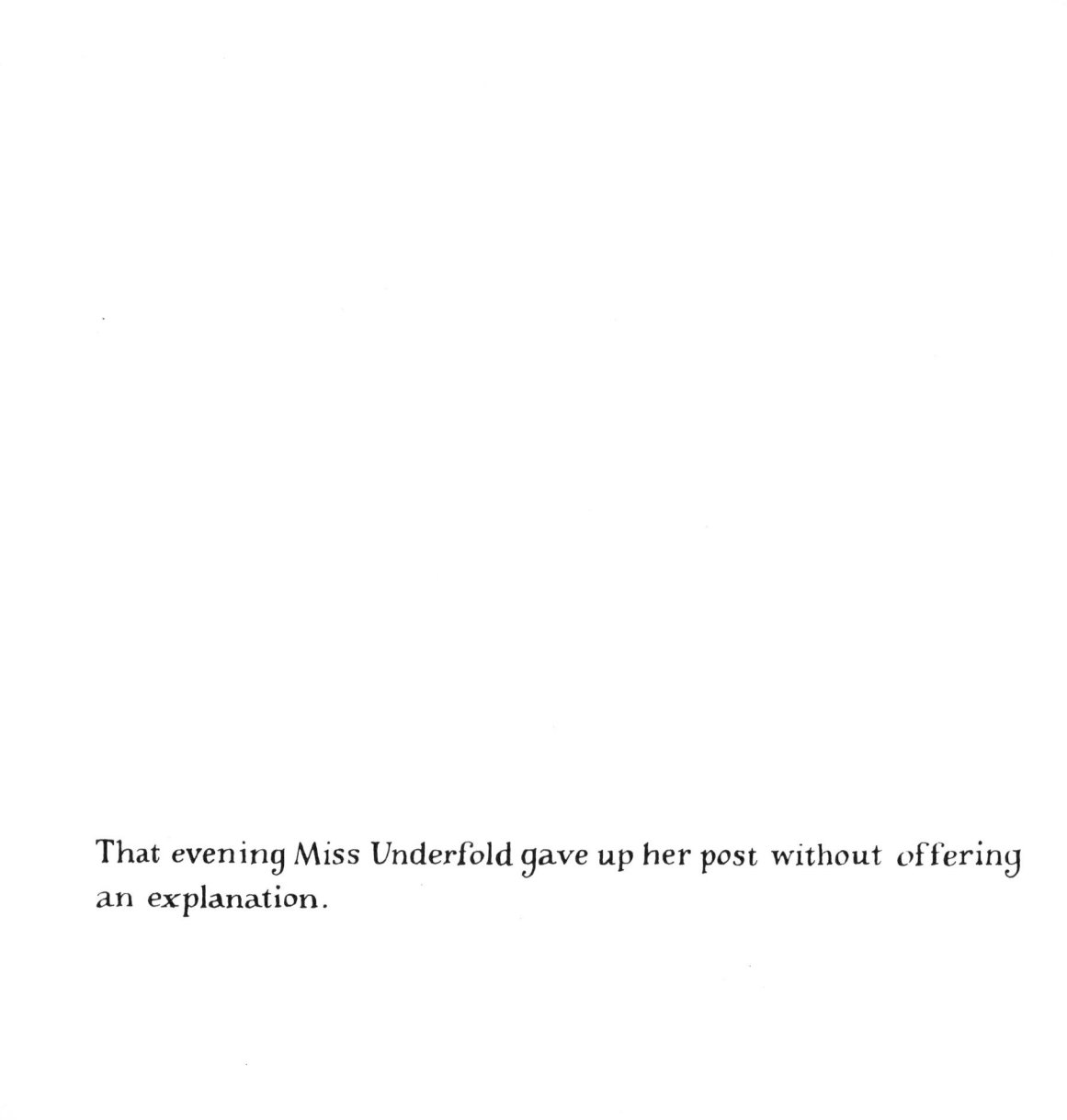

That evening Miss Underfold gave up her post without offering an explanation.

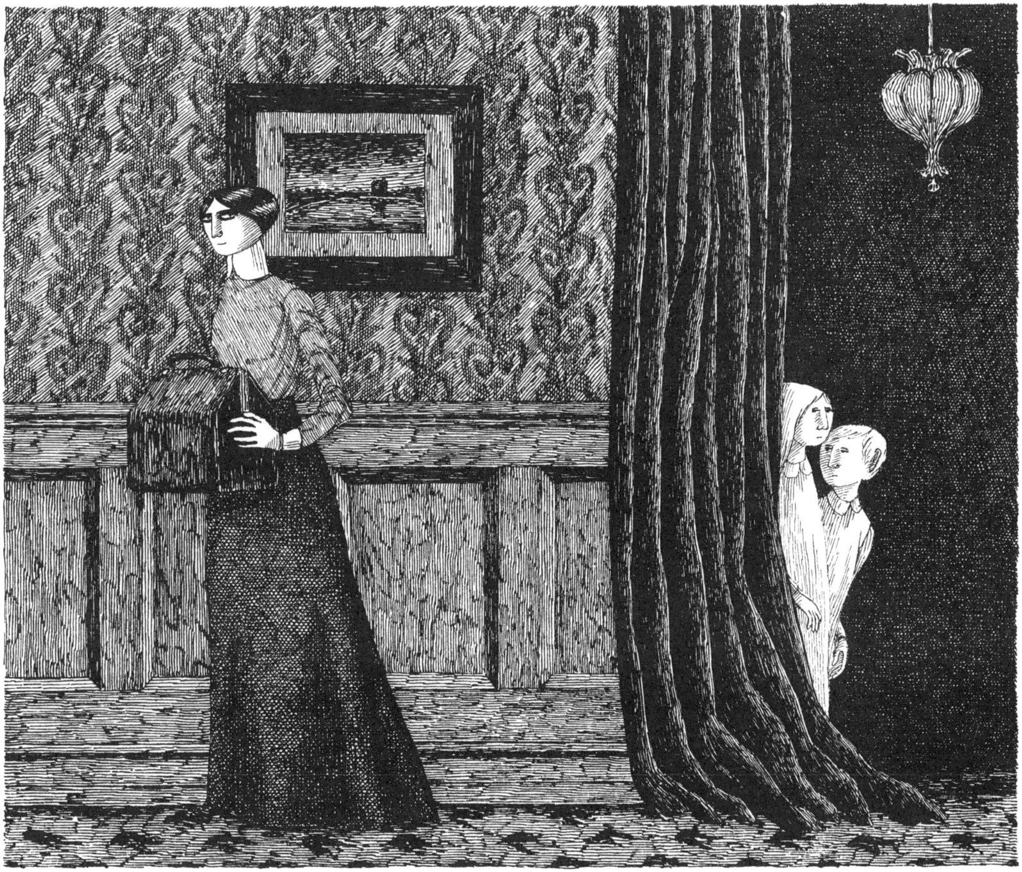

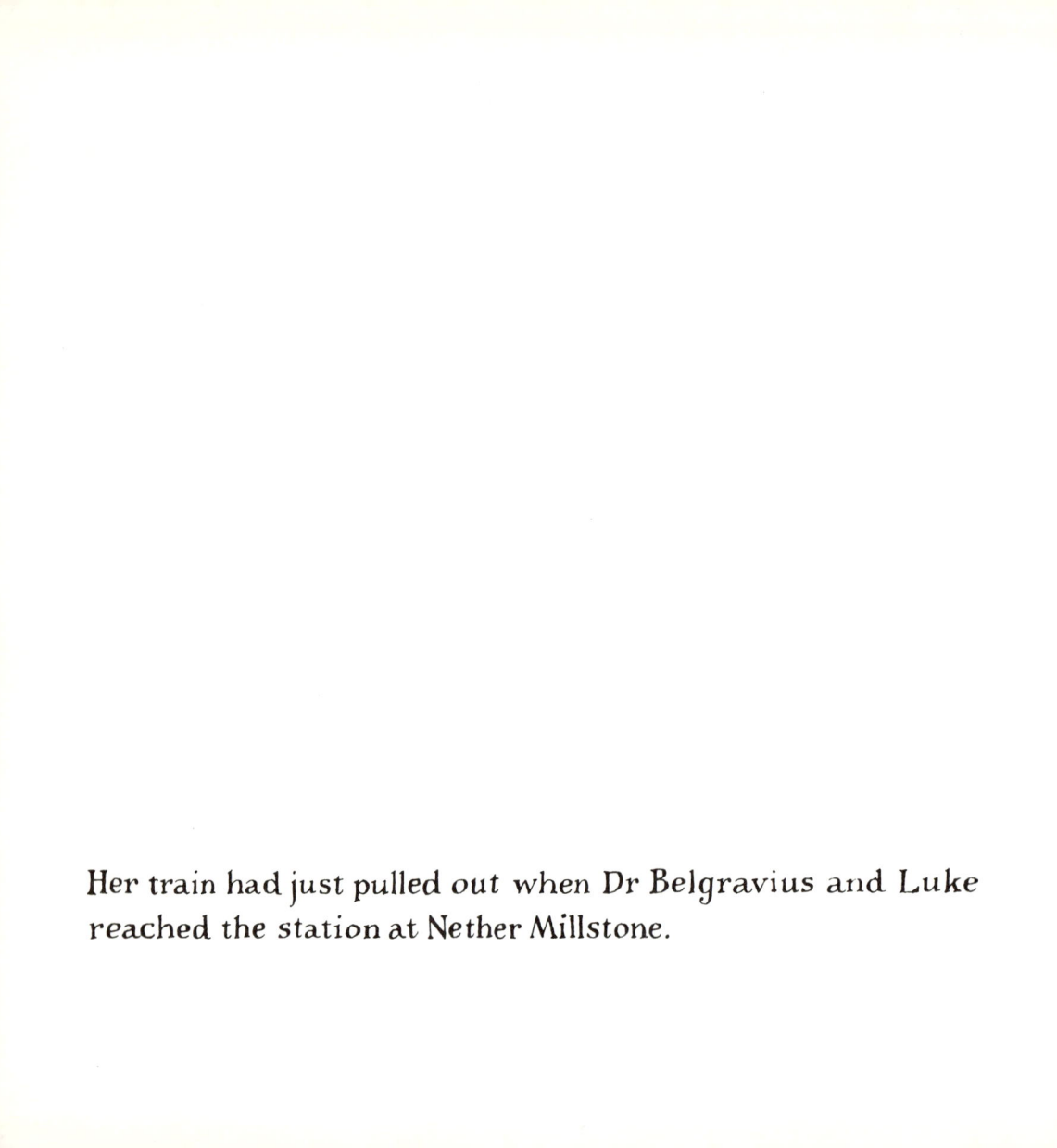

Her train had just pulled out when Dr Belgravius and Luke reached the station at Nether Millstone.

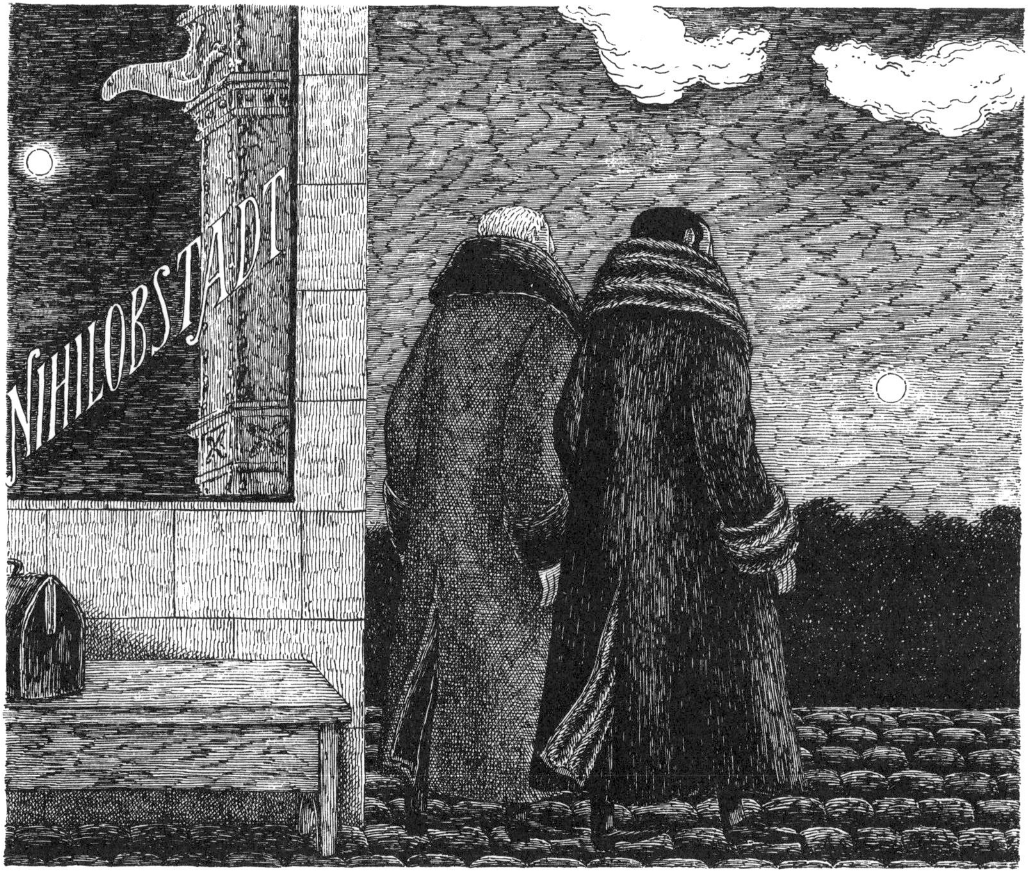
NIHILOBSTADT

She was met at the terminus in London by a friend.

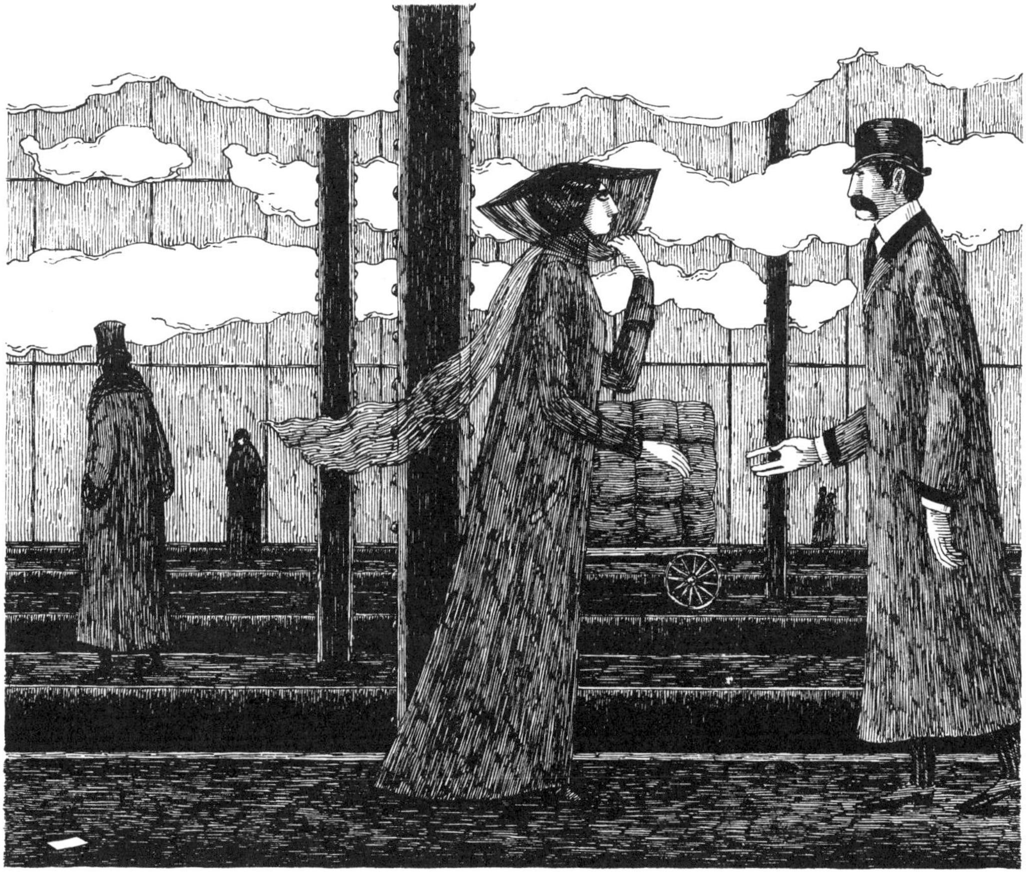

A letter to Lady Isobel from St Clot mentioned that Horace Gollop had been paralysed for over a year now.

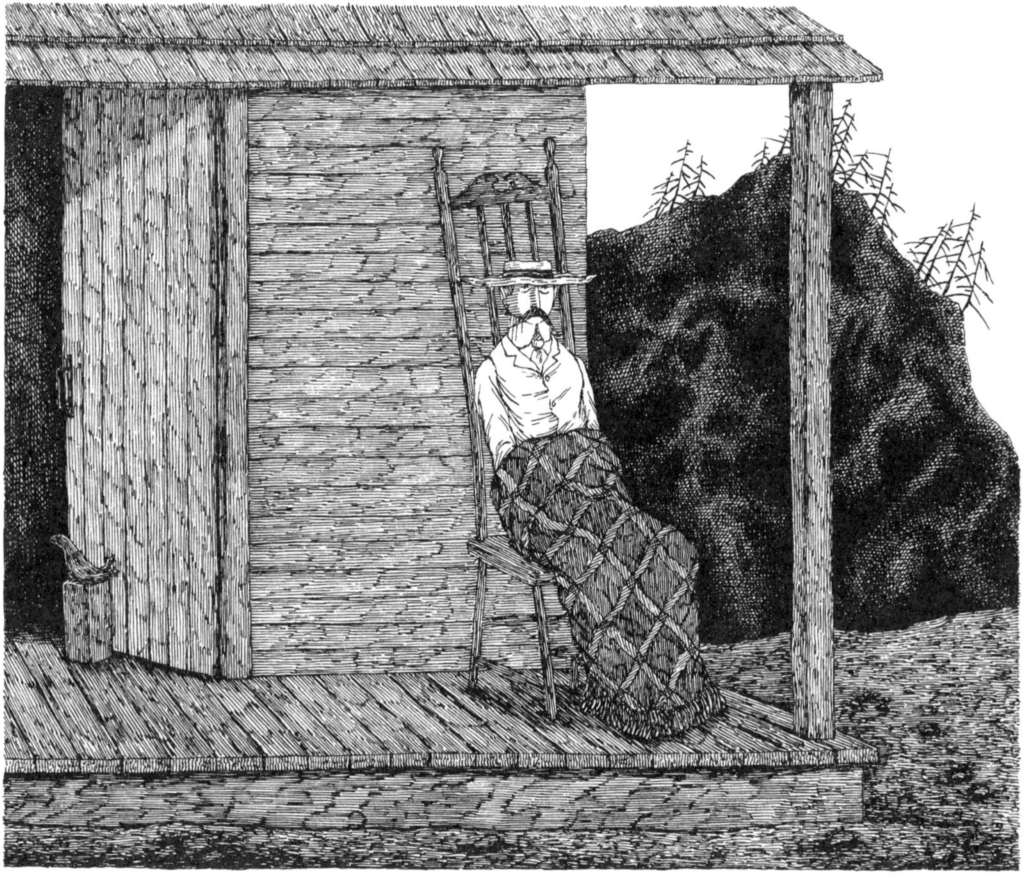

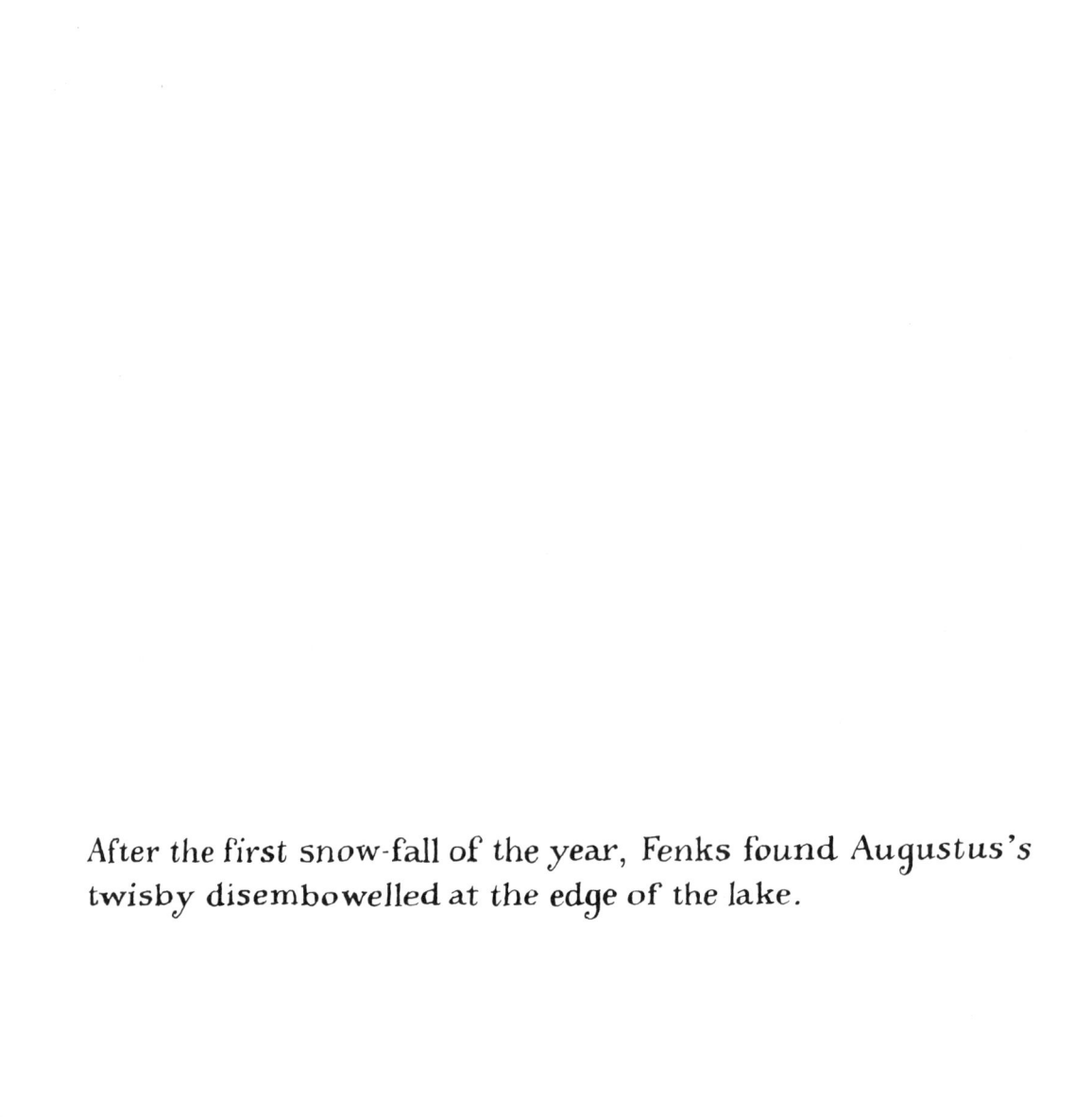

After the first snow-fall of the year, Fenks found Augustus's twisby disembowelled at the edge of the lake.

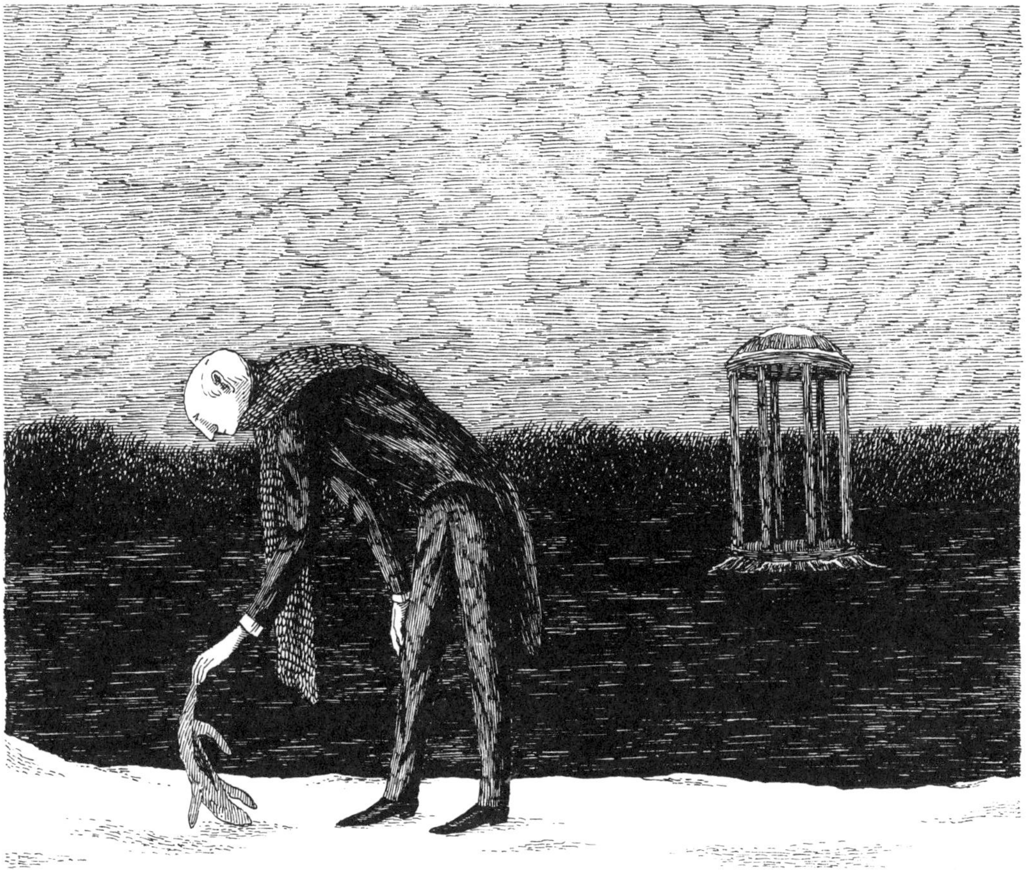

The next evening Mr MacAbloo delivered a lecture on the Seroulian Heresy at a bethel in the slums.

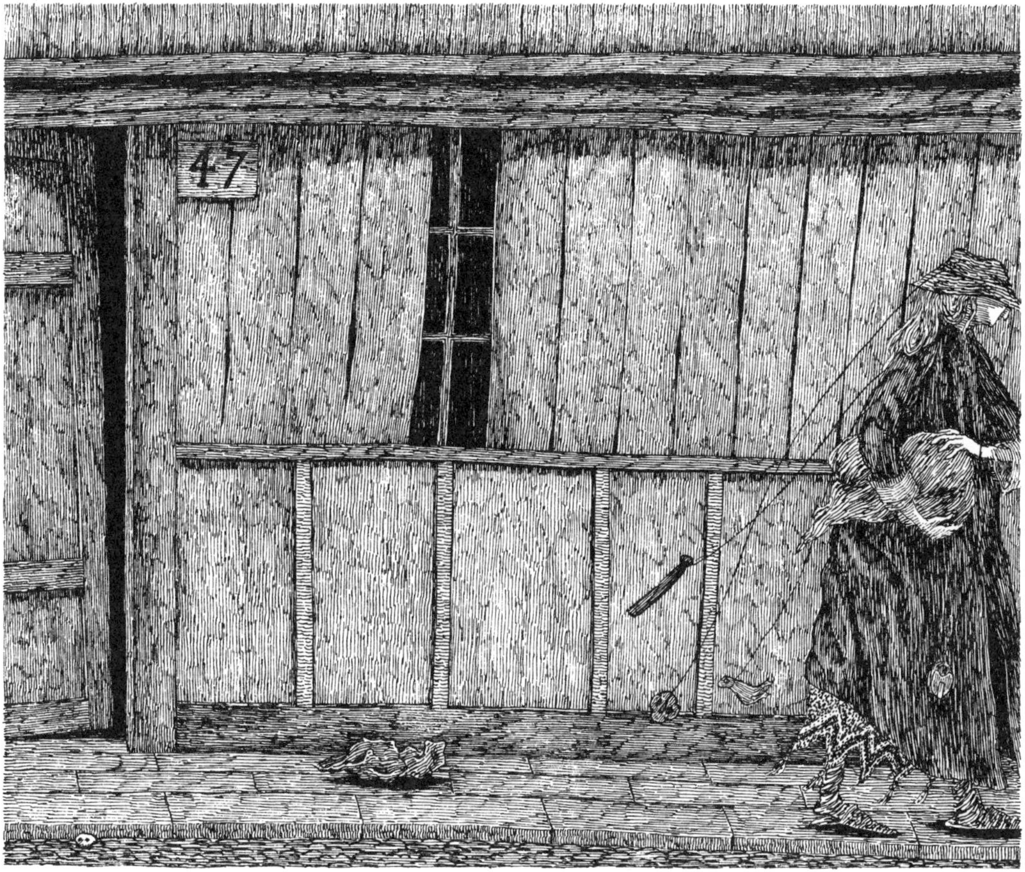
47

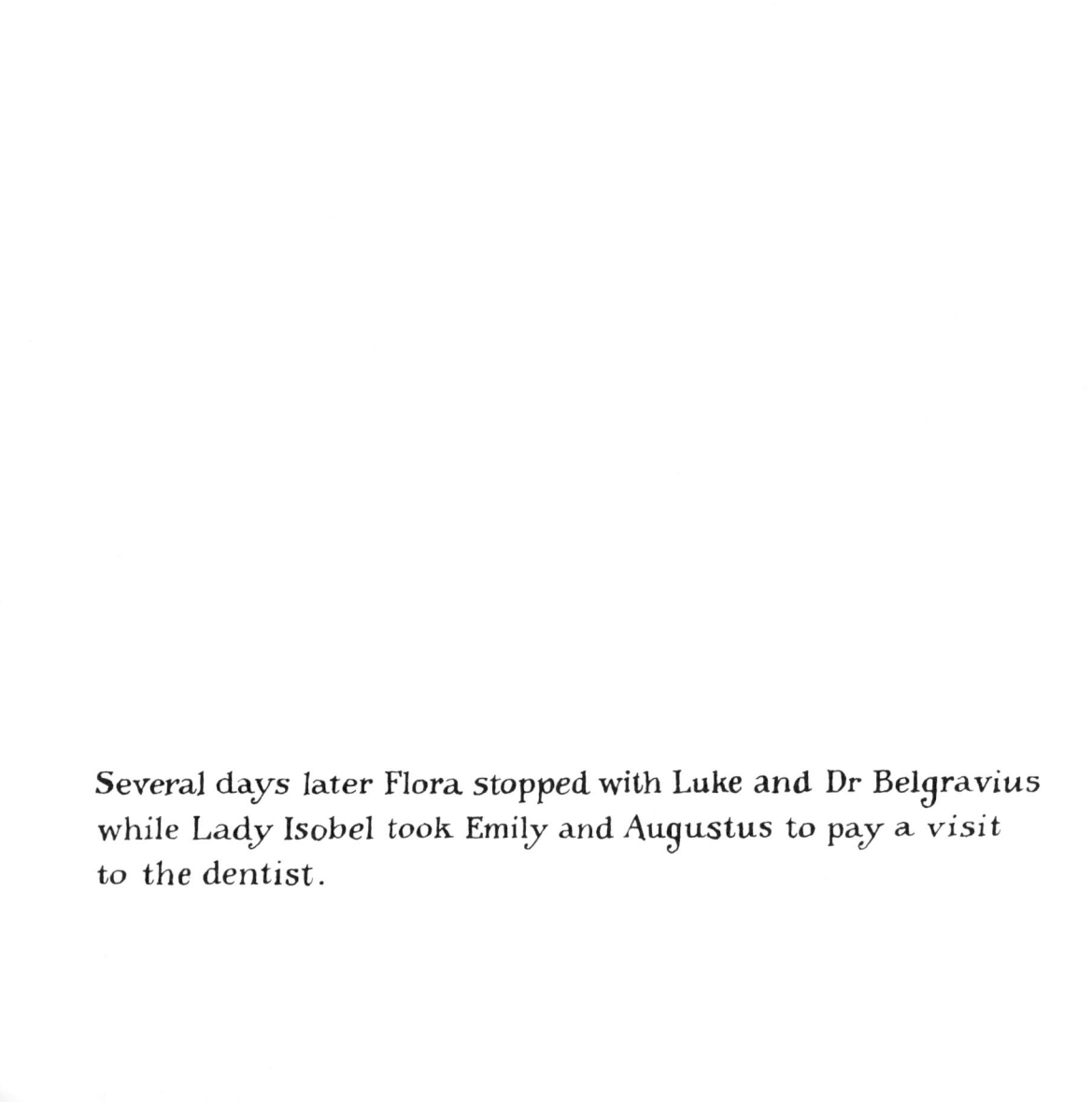

Several days later Flora stopped with Luke and Dr Belgravius while Lady Isobel took Emily and Augustus to pay a visit to the dentist.

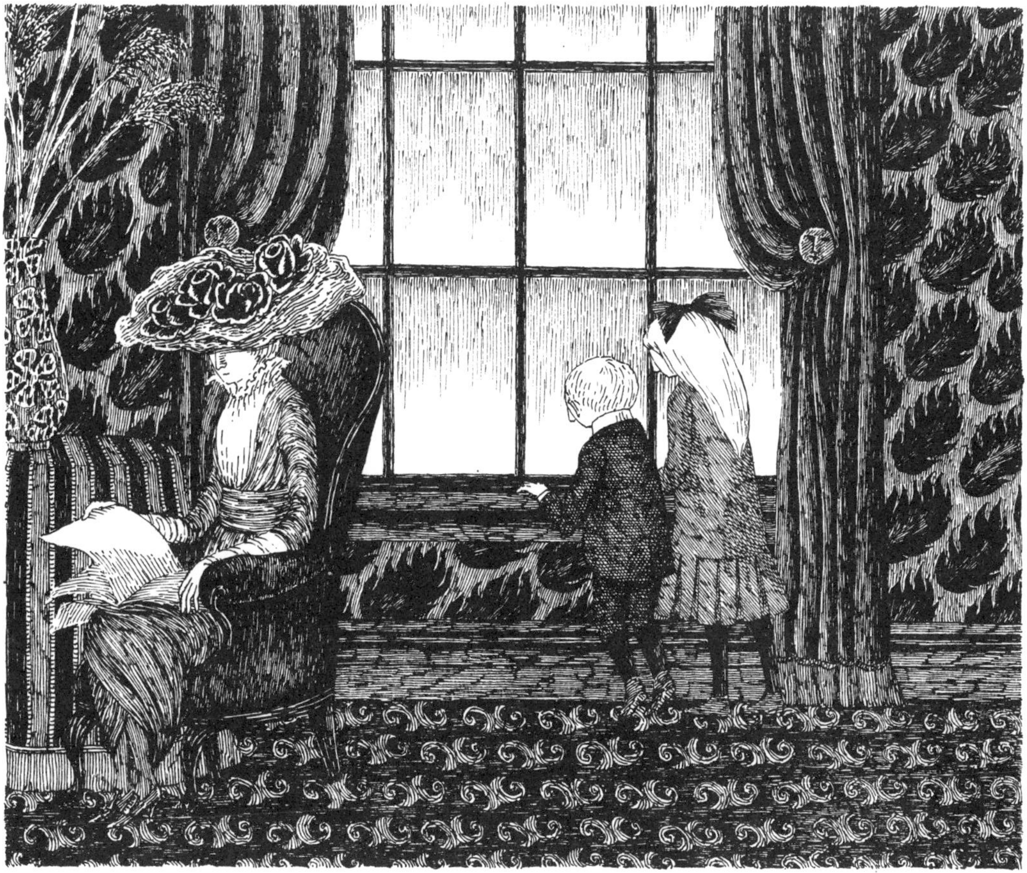

During tea the children said that from the window of his waiting room they had seen Miss Underfold wearing a hat decorated with black lilies.

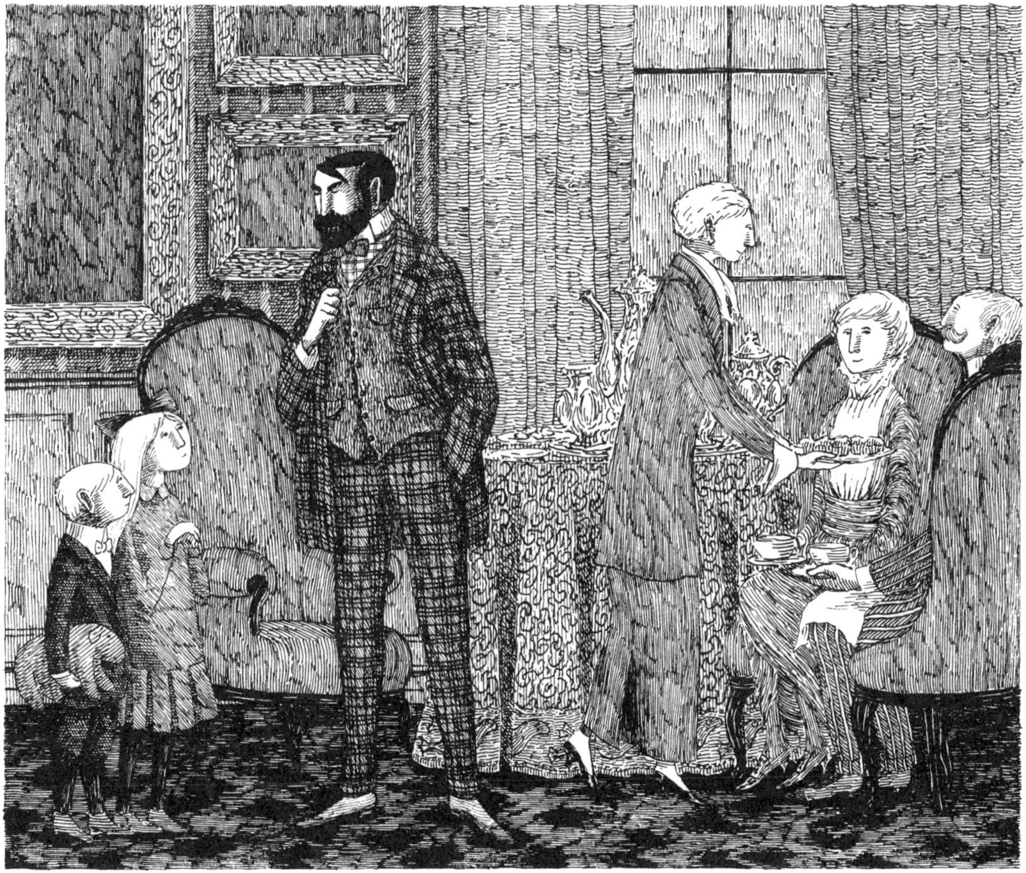

At the same time, in the Soiled Dove, Victoria Scone danced a tango with Horace Gollop.

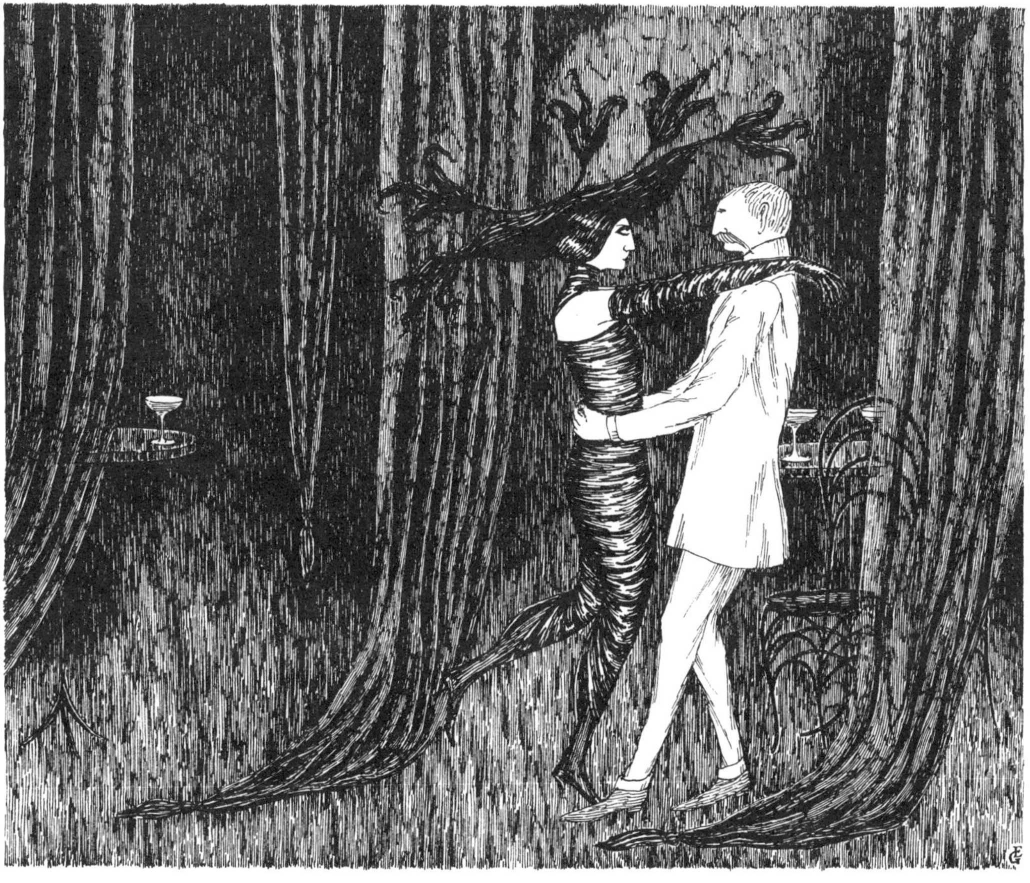